Which cowboy will become the first daddy in Cactus, Texas?

Their moms want grandchildren—
and these conniving matchmakers will
stop at nothing to turn their cowboy
sons into family men!
Who'll be the first to fall?

Cal Baxter
or
Spence Hauk
or
Tuck Langford
or
Mac Gibbons

4 TOTS for 4 TEXANS

P9-CSF-058

Dear Reader,

After the Randalls, I didn't think I'd find four men as lovable, or hardheaded, as those cowboys. But as I turned to my native Texas for inspiration, lo and behold, there they were. Not brothers, but best friends for life.

Cal, Spence, Tuck and Mac grew up together in a small West Texas town. Oil on their family properties could have made it easy for them, but they've worked hard all their lives. They know the value of work...and friendship. Nothing can come between them, especially women. In fact, they'd vowed long ago not to marry. Or to kiss girls, either, but Tuck dismissed that promise when he was thirteen. It didn't take the others long to agree. Their bodies hardened by a tough, outdoor life, their eyes keen, their hearts filled with loyalty and honesty, these four draw women like pie on a hot summer day draws flies.

But their mothers, with only one chick apiece, want grandchildren. The other ladies in town have babies to cuddle. Why don't they? And they set out to do something about it.

I hope you enjoy these four guys and their fall for four special women. I certainly did. But don't you stampede to Texas looking for men like these. They may be out there, but we Texas ladies aren't looking to give them away!

Judy Christenberry

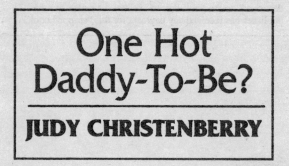

One Hot
Daddy-To-Be?

JUDY CHRISTENBERRY

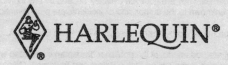

HARLEQUIN®

TORONTO • NEW YORK • LONDON
AMSTERDAM • PARIS • SYDNEY • HAMBURG
STOCKHOLM • ATHENS • TOKYO • MILAN • MADRID
PRAGUE • WARSAW • BUDAPEST • AUCKLAND

If you purchased this book without a cover you should be aware
that this book is stolen property. It was reported as "unsold and
destroyed" to the publisher, and neither the author nor the
publisher has received any payment for this "stripped book."

ISBN 0-373-16773-3

ONE HOT DADDY-TO-BE?

Copyright © 1999 by Judy Russell Christenberry.

All rights reserved. Except for use in any review, the reproduction or
utilization of this work in whole or in part in any form by any electronic,
mechanical or other means, now known or hereafter invented, including
xerography, photocopying and recording, or in any information storage
or retrieval system, is forbidden without the written permission of the
publisher, Harlequin Enterprises Limited, 225 Duncan Mill Road,
Don Mills, Ontario, Canada M3B 3K9.

All characters in this book have no existence outside the imagination of
the author and have no relation whatsoever to anyone bearing the same
name or names. They are not even distantly inspired by any individual
known or unknown to the author, and all incidents are pure invention.

This edition published by arrangement with Harlequin Books S.A.

® and TM are trademarks of the publisher. Trademarks indicated with
® are registered in the United States Patent and Trademark Office, the
Canadian Trade Marks Office and in other countries.

Look us up on-line at: http://www.romance.net

Printed in U.S.A.

Prologue

Mabel Baxter dealt the cards in rapid-fire fashion, from long practice, and talked at the same time. "Can you believe it? I ran into Henrietta at the grocery store yesterday. She's got another grandbaby on the way!"

"That makes three for her," Edith Hauk said, her voice filled with frustration.

"Luisa Ann has five," Ruth Langford said as she sorted her cards. Her carefully styled blond hair, dyed to hide the gray, never moved as she shook her head.

"Even Thelma Morehouse has one on the way," Florence Gibbons pointed out. "One heart."

Edith studied her cards before saying, "Two diamonds. It's just not fair. All our boys are more handsome than Thelma's. Why, that Morehouse boy couldn't walk and chew gum at the same time when he was a teenager."

Florence sighed. "It's not a question of their attractiveness, Edith. You know that. They're all handsome and eligible, good providers. And stubborn as mules." She was the youngest of the four women and kept her brown hair, minus the gray, of course, short and curly.

Mabel spoke up. "I think it's because there are four of them." She drummed her long nails into the table as she considered her words. The nails, carefully tended, were her pride and joy. "Ever since Mac came back to town, they've done everything together."

"You're not blaming Mac, are you?" Florence asked, her defenses up. "He at least tried marriage. It's not his fault it didn't work out."

"A'course not. But they always have a foursome to do things together. Ever since grade school. If one or two of them got married, then the others would, too."

"And we'd have grandbabies," Ruth said with a sigh.

Florence shook her head. "Wishing isn't going to make it happen."

"Neither is anything else," Mabel complained. "We're all gonna die without seeing our grandbabies born."

"Not me," Florence calmly said. "Your bid, Ruth."

Instead of bidding, Ruth leaned across the table. "That's easy for you to say, Florence Gibbons. Mac isn't your son."

Florence slapped her cards facedown on the table. "He's as good as my son and you know it, Ruth Langford. My brother-in-law and his wife died when Mac was ten. I raised him. He's mine."

Edith hurriedly soothed her friend. "You know

Ruth didn't intend to upset you. What did you mean, 'not you'?"

"I've got a plan."

Florence's statement put an end to any interest in the bridge game.

"To get Mac married again? How? What are you going to do?" Mabel asked.

The center of attention slowly picked up her cards, not looking at the others. "I'm not tellin', but I'm not sittin' around waiting for fate to step in. The boy has been alone long enough."

Silence followed her words.

Then Mabel slammed her palm down on the table. "Well, if Flo can get Mac married, I reckon I can do the same with Cal...somehow."

"Shoot, I'm not gonna be the only one with an empty cradle," Ruth said.

"But what are you going to do?" Edith demanded, fingering the diamond heart pendant, a gift from her husband, she always wore. "We can't hog-tie 'em and drag 'em to the altar. And it's not like there are a lot of eligible ladies here in Cactus."

Florence smiled and rearranged her cards.

"Flo knows something," Ruth said, her gaze sharpening.

The lady's bland look told them all Ruth's words were true, but she refused to respond to their questions.

After her cohorts subsided, Florence looked up. "We could make everything a little more interesting."

"What does that mean?" Edith demanded.

"A little bet. Say, whoever gets a grandchild first wins a prize."

"What prize?" Mabel wanted to know.

"Um, something good. How about a week at the Green House?" Neiman-Marcus's famous spa was popular with the oil-rich ladies of Cactus.

"You mean, the other three foot the bill?" Ruth asked, her eyes narrowing in calculation.

"That's right. Might as well have a prize worth winning. Besides the grandbaby, that is. And you could do a bit of shopping for the new family addition on the way home." Florence smiled again, as if she were supremely confident, something she knew would drive her friends crazy.

"You're on," Mabel said, her teeth clenched.

"It's a deal," Ruth and Edith agreed together.

"Good," Florence responded. "Ruth, it's your bid."

Chapter One

"You know…" Tuck Langford said, his Western drawl only a part of the picture he made as he leaned his chair back on its two hind legs and tipped his cowboy hat up with the bottle of beer he held. "She might make winning the bet worthwhile."

His three friends stared at him.

On good weather Saturdays, the four of them, along with a few other old friends, held a rodeo at one of their nearby ranches, riding wild horses and bulls. Then, holding to tradition, they retreated to The Old Cantina, a Mexican restaurant in the small Texas town of Cactus, located between Lubbock and the New Mexico border.

"What are you talking about?" Cal Baxter, the sheriff of Cactus, demanded, though he thought he knew as he followed Tuck's gaze.

"I'm talkin' about Jess," Tuck responded.

"I know you're talking about Jess. But I don't like to hear you referring to her as some…some prize."

"I don't get why you've never made a move on her, Cal," Mac Gibbons demanded, introducing an entirely new topic. "You've warned us away from her for years."

"Hell, it'd be like taking my little sister to bed," Cal returned, a fierce frown on his face. He didn't like this conversation much.

The fourth member of their long-held friendship, Spencer Hauk, roused himself from the trance he'd fallen into, thinking about his success with a bull he'd long battled. "What are y'all talking about? A bet or Jessica?"

"Both," Tuck said.

"No, we're not," Cal insisted. "Jess has nothing to do with a bet."

"Yes, she does," Tuck returned. "Well, not really, I guess, except that she qualifies since she's female and young enough to have kids."

"What in the hell are you talking about?" Mac demanded.

"I'm talking about our blessed mothers," Tuck added cryptically.

Spence put his empty beer bottle on the table and waved to their waitress. "Man, I don't talk about women and my mother in the same sentence. She likes to believe I'm still, uh, inexperienced."

"Quiet, Spence," Cal said. "We don't want to discuss your sex life. We want to know what Tuck is talking about." Cal leaned forward and stared at Tuck. "Let's quit being mysterious. What *are* you talking about?"

Tuck laughed. "Always the sheriff, Cal. You've got to get to the bottom of everything. If you'd ever visit your mother, you'd know." He let a superior

smile rest on his lips. He'd visited his mother yesterday.

"Get on with it," Cal growled.

"Okay, but you're not going to like it." He took
a last drink from his beer and set it next to Spence's.
"Our mothers have made a bet about who will get
the first grandchild."

The other three frowned at each other and then all
stared at Tuck.

Mac, with his legal background, made the first
statement. "But none of us is married."

"True," Tuck agreed. "And I don't recall being
married as being part of the bet. Though I suspect
they'd prefer that we do it legally."

"Your mother told you this?" Cal demanded, suspicion in his gaze.

"Not only told me, but she also offered me a
bribe."

All three of his listeners shoved their seats back
from the table, as if distancing themselves from the
entire subject.

"No way," Cal said.

"Won't happen," Spence insisted.

"Been there, done that. Never again," Mac added.

Tuck sat there, smiling.

Then Cal recalled his original statement. "You're
talking about getting *Jessica* pregnant?" He sounded
as if his friend had suggested blowing up the world.

"Nope. I just said she might be worth the effort."

"You stay away from her," Cal growled.

"There you go again, Cal," Mac interjected. "If
you want her, why aren't you doing anything about

it? And if you don't want her, why do you work so hard to keep us away from her?''

"Hell, don't you remember? We vowed to avoid the marriage trap. You've warned us enough times." That response, as true as it was, would direct the conversation away from Jessica, he hoped. He didn't want any close examination of his relationship with her.

"I didn't mean to— Well, I was speaking from experience. I didn't mean your marriages would turn out bad," Mac explained, frowning.

"We took a vow," Cal said again.

"We were eleven at the time," Tuck reminded him with a laugh. "We weren't going to kiss any girls, either."

Even Cal relaxed at that reminder. "So we were a little overly enthusiastic. But that doesn't mean I'm going to jump into marriage to please my mother. And kids? I don't think so."

Spence looked a little dreamy-eyed, but Cal figured it might be because of the beer. "Someday, I want a son." Then, after a quick glance at his friends, he added, "But not now. Definitely not now."

The waitress finally reached their table and another round of beers was ordered. "Your nachos will be right out."

Tuck nodded and gave her a friendly smile. "Say, when Jess finishes in the kitchen, tell her to stop by, okay?"

"Sure. You're not going to complain about me, are you, cowboy?"

"Nah, Nita. You're doin' a bang-up job," Tuck assured her before she left the table.

"Why did you do that?" Cal demanded, pulling his chair closer and glaring at his friend.

"I haven't seen Jess in a while. Thought we should say hello, be friendly," Tuck assured him, an innocent look on his face.

"Being friendly with the ladies is one of your major talents, you mangy dog," Cal growled. "Jess isn't that kind of lady, though."

Before their argument could escalate, a beautiful woman arrived at their table. Cal stared at Jessica Hoya as if seeing her for the first time. Her jet-black hair attested to her Mexican-American mother, but her green eyes and fine features were from her white father. He knew she attracted men's attention. Hell, he'd dedicated his life to ensuring those men kept their distance.

"You wanted to see me, Tuck?" Her voice was pure velvet, making a man think of dark nights and satin sheets.

"Hey, Jess, long time no see." He stood as he spoke, which had the other three scrambling to their feet.

"Take your seats, boys. I didn't mean to disturb you. Nita said you wanted to speak to me?" she said to Tuck as the men sat down again.

"Haven't seen you in a while. I wondered what you've been up to." Tuck smiled.

She put one hand on her trim waist and grinned at one of Cal's best friends. "I've been avoiding layabouts like you. I'm a businesswoman, you know."

"Yeah. I heard you're a real success now."

She sighed. "Yeah, a real success."

Cal studied her, noticing how tired she looked.

Was something wrong? He'd always told her to come to him if she had any difficulties. "Jess? Is there a problem?"

She flashed him a brief look with her green eyes before addressing Tuck again. "I'm busy with the new restaurants, Tuck. It doesn't leave me a lot of time to play."

Cal frowned. She was fixing all her attention on Tuck. Was she interested in him? How come he'd never noticed it before?

"You must be finding *some* time. I heard you were seeing Johnny Boyd," Tuck continued.

Cal almost broke the arms off his chair as his grip tightened. He hadn't heard that rumor. Why hadn't Tuck told him? "Jess, is he right? That man's no good." His gray eyes darkened as they glared at her. "I'm telling you—stay away from him."

JESSICA CROSSED HER ARMS in front of her, "It's none of your business, Cal, or Tuck's, either. I'm an adult, remember?"

Not only was she an adult, she was a proven veteran in the tough restaurant business. But Cal never could admit that she'd grown up. To him, she was still a four-year-old, following his every step, fascinated with his every move. Of course, she admitted ruefully, she still was fascinated by him. But she was no longer a child.

Abruptly he stood and pulled her by the arm over to a window, away from the table. Leaning in, he stormed, "Baby, you have to be careful. Men are— some men are only out for what they can get."

"Do *not* call me 'baby,' and please don't insult

my intelligence by telling me something I learned at my mother's knee.'' She pulled from his grasp, glaring at him. This man drove her crazy!

"I know you think you're all grown up, baby, but—"

Frustration boiled over. Jessica had had Cal as a protector from the time she was four, he an older eight. Her mother, abandoned by her wealthy lover before Jessica was born, had supported herself by cleaning houses.

When oil struck the town twenty-four years ago, a lot more ladies had been able to afford help, and pay more for it. Mrs. Baxter, Cal's mother, had been one of them. And she hadn't objected when Jessica had accompanied her mother.

Cal, an only child, had immediately adopted Jessica as his little sister.

He allowed her to follow him on his adventures, teaching her how to climb trees, ride horses and obey his every command. He still thought she should do the latter. It wasn't that he gave bad advice. It was that she no longer was a little girl. And she no longer wanted to be his sister.

"I think I deserve a social life. I've been working too hard lately."

He frowned again. "Your restaurant is in trouble?"

She rolled her eyes. "My restaurants are fine. More than fine. But they take a lot of work."

"I didn't mean you shouldn't relax and have fun, but Johnny—"

She interrupted him. "So who do you suggest I play with, if not Johnny?" She had him now. She was sure he wouldn't suggest anyone who hadn't been dead for a decade.

"Uh, what about Susie Crawford? You used to hang around with her. Or—"

"Male, Cal. Male company. I'm not looking for girlfriends." She'd been trying to convince herself she could love—care about someone else. Anyone else but Cal Baxter. So far she'd been miserably unsuccessful.

"Now, baby, you've got plenty of time before you need to be thinking along those lines. You're still young—"

"I'm twenty-seven, Cal. My clock is ticking."

"Clock? Clock! You mean, you want to have a baby? Jess, you wouldn't— I mean, it worked out okay for your mother, but it would be hard for you."

Her cheeks flamed. "I didn't mean I wanted to be an unwed mother! I want to have a husband, a family. I want to belong." She regretted the yearning in her voice. She didn't want to appear weak in front of Cal.

"Baby, you belong to the Baxters. You know that. You're family."

Which brought her right back to her problem. She wasn't really a part of their family. And she never would be. Her childish dreams of marrying Cal Baxter would never happen. If for no other reason than he still thought she was a baby.

A baby? Well, she thought, suddenly determined to teach him a lesson, she'd show him. She leaned closer and before he could start another lecture, one demonstrating how much she needed to follow his advice, she slid her arms around his neck and locked her lips with his.

She'd had longer kisses, kisses that involved a lot more body parts, kisses definitely in less public places. But she'd never had a kiss that shook her more.

Determined to keep it casual, in spite of the trembling that filled her, she pulled back and grinned into Cal's shocked face. "Number one, I am not a baby. Number two, you are not my brother, my father, my protector...or anything else. Got it, big guy?"

He continued to stare at her as if she'd stripped in front of him.

Retreat seemed the best choice. With a wave to the other three, she walked sedately to the kitchen.

CAL DIDN'T MOVE. He was afraid his body wouldn't obey his commands. Or, if he moved at all, he'd end up chasing Jess to the kitchen.

What had gotten into her?

"Cal, you okay?" Spence demanded, appearing beside him.

"Huh? Uh, yeah," he assured his friend, clearing his throat. What had the woman done to him? He could scarcely speak.

"The nachos are here. Come back to the table."

"Sure." The only way to survive what had happened was to erase it from memory. Forget about those soft lips that caressed his, forget about the lithe, sexy body so close to his. Forget that Jessica, little Jessica, had kissed him.

He grabbed his beer bottle as soon as he reached

the table and swigged down half of it before he even settled in his chair.

Mac frowned at him. "You okay, Cal?"

"Yeah, fine." He didn't look at any of them.

"I guess Jess has grown up," Tuck teased.

"Shut up!" Cal roared, fire in his eyes.

"Have a nacho," Spence said, scooting the big tray toward Cal. "Say, did you see the way that guy from the Double X ranch rode old Whiteface today? He's good."

The other two followed his lead, returning their conversation to a review of their rodeo. Cal vaguely heard the discussion going on around him, but he didn't join in.

He needed to talk to Jessica. Something was going on or she wouldn't have reacted that way. He'd been taking care of her for a lot of years. Of course, there were those three years when he'd gone to Dallas and worked for the FBI that she'd been on her own.

But he'd been back for four years now. She'd never done anything like that kiss before. She'd been happy for him when he'd come back to take his father's place as sheriff. In fact, she'd hugged him.

Suddenly he realized that hug had been almost as startling as her kiss today. He'd avoided thinking about it, but holding her in his arms that day, after being away from her, had shocked him.

She was definitely a woman.

Her breasts had flattened against his chest. Her scent had surrounded him, one he'd unconsciously associated with her for a long time. The purity of gardenias. White, delicate, beautiful. Her arms, slender, fragile, had shown strength as they'd wrapped themselves around his neck.

He'd immediately backed away and tried to wipe the happening from his mind. But it had hidden there, deep in his head, waiting to jump out at him. He'd noticed her delicious curves from that day on.

And had avoided her.

But in a small town like Cactus, it was impossible.

Suddenly he leaned forward and interrupted the conversation.

"Where did you hear she was dating Johnny Boyd?"

Tuck chuckled. "I wondered if you'd heard anything. It's just a rumor."

"Damn it, you should've told me!" Cal raged. "That man's not worth spit, and you know it."

"Some women like those kind," Tuck said gently, pity in his gaze.

"Why are you looking at me like that?"

Tuck shrugged his shoulders. "I guess because we've stood fast for a lot of years. I hate to see things change."

"Nothing's changing!" Cal snapped. He couldn't let things change. Especially when it concerned Jessica. He was her protector...not a predator like Johnny.

"Want another beer?" Spence asked.

Cal jerked his gaze to Spence, catching the same look on his face, though not as obvious as Tuck's. "No! I don't want another beer. I want to know why you're all lookin' at me like I'd been bested by a mama skunk."

Mac slapped him on the shoulder. "Don't worry, Cal. We'll stand by you."

"Stand by me for what?" His friends were acting weird.

"Because, Cal," Tuck informed him, his face suddenly turning serious. "I reckon you're going to win that stupid contest, after all."

Chapter Two

Jessica plastered her body against the cool adobe wall of the restaurant kitchen and took deep, gulping breaths. Oh, man, her impulsiveness had sure gotten her in a pickle now.

All this time, she'd told herself her feelings for Cal were part of her childhood and could be easily dismissed. She'd told herself she couldn't be in love with him. Touching him now had been the biggest mistake she'd ever made in her twenty-seven years. It was going to take a lot more work to convince herself now.

Not that she hadn't touched him before.

But not...not sexually. Not since she'd first realized what the differences between boys and girls really were. Not since she'd started wanting him with all her heart.

Nita pushed open the kitchen door.

"Jess? Your guest is here."

Jessica stepped away from the wall, hoping her trembling legs would hold her, and trying to gather her composure. If she hadn't agreed to meet Alex here, she would've gone away, as far away as she could.

"Thanks, Nita. Bring us some nachos and two diet Cokes. Then we'll order."

"You got it," the waitress agreed, backing out of the kitchen.

"Uh, Nita, have...have the guys left yet?"

No one in the kitchen had to ask who "the guys" were.

From the time she'd opened her first restaurant, the four men had been regular customers. Supporting their friend, they'd always said. And eating a lot of nachos.

"Not yet. They're doing a lot of talking today and not much eating. They haven't even ordered their dinner."

Nita had been in the dining room when Jessica had made her huge mistake. There was a curiosity in the waitress's gaze that made Jessica glad she was the boss. Nita wouldn't dare ask her about her bizarre behavior. "Thanks."

Nita left, and Jessica ignored the stares from the staff. "Be on your toes," she teased with a weak smile. "I'm going to order everything on the menu."

Then, squaring her shoulders, she marched into the dining room, keeping her gaze fixed on the lobby. She didn't want to face Cal yet.

Alexandra Logan, a sophisticated blonde from Dallas, was waiting in the lobby. Her navy-blue business suit made her stand out among the denimed diners in Cactus.

Jessica stepped forward and kissed her cheek.

"Welcome to Cactus, Alex. Sorry I couldn't meet you in Dallas."

"No problem. With the offer that's on the table, my boss had no trouble with me driving this far."

Jessica frowned, but she led the way to a small table in the back corner of the restaurant. Fortunately, it happened to be on the other side of the room from her four friends, but she imagined she felt their gazes on her and Alex.

Of course. They were the four most eligible bachelors in town. Each man had broad shoulders and a handsome face. When they smiled, half the ladies in Cactus swooned. While she thought Cal, with his sandy hair and gray eyes, was the most attractive, the other three had their supporters in that category.

So, they were a little spoiled. And they checked out every woman as if they had first choice. Which they pretty much did.

"Are we drawing a lot of attention, or am I just imagining it?" Alex asked as she sat across from Jessica.

"Don't worry about it. There's just a lot of testosterone floating around today."

Alex casually surveyed the room. "You're right about that. And that foursome over there is pretty awesome."

"Don't ever let them hear you say that. They're too full of themselves as it is," Jessica said with a smile. Still, she tried to follow Alex's gaze, to see if it was Cal she made eye contact with. Did she find him the most attractive?— No, she told herself, it was none of her business.

"Well," she said, clearing her throat, "shall we get down to business?"

Her suggestion was ignored for the moment as Nita set their drinks and a tray of nachos on the table.

Alex daintily sniffed the air. "No wonder you've been so successful, Jess. These smell wonderful."

"They're the best in the west," Nita pronounced with a smile. "Let me know when you're ready to order," she said before leaving.

"You mean, we're going to eat more after these?"

Jessica smiled. She loved it when someone praised her business. It was her child, her only family. "I told you I'm good. Just wait until you try our fajitas."

"I'm going to have to diet for a week to make up for this meal." Alex flashed her a dazzling smile. "But it'll be worth it."

"Hey, Jess, aren't you going to introduce your guest to your old friends?" Tuck asked, suddenly appearing at their table and staring at Alex.

Jessica should have expected Tuck's approach. He wasn't a man to let a good-looking woman go unappreciated. "Alex, this is Tucker Langford." Jessica watched as Tuck took Alex's hand and held it a bit longer than necessary. "Tuck, this is my attorney, Alexandra Logan."

The measuring yet flirtatious look the two exchanged amused Jessica. And relieved her a little, too. She didn't mind Alex being interested in Tuck.

"An attorney, huh? You're the prettiest attorney I've ever seen," Tuck drawled.

"Thank you, Mr. Langford. You're the best-looking cowboy I've ever seen. You are a cowboy, aren't you?'' Alex asked, giving him an up-and-down look that would've rocked most men.

''Yes, ma'am, I am.''

Jessica leaned forward. ''When Tuck first showed up to play football when he was twelve, he was wearing cowboy boots. The coach had to work long and hard to get him to change to athletic shoes.''

Tuck grinned and shrugged. ''They were my best boots.'' Before Alex could respond, other than smiling, he added, ''I've been sent over here to ask you ladies to join us. We're just now getting around to ordering. We thought the company of the two prettiest ladies in the room would make our food taste better.''

Jessica felt her stomach sink. She couldn't face Cal again so soon. She'd hoped to avoid him for a week or two...or however long it took for him to forget she'd kissed him.

Alex, on the other hand, appeared intrigued with Tuck. Not a surprise, Jessica thought. She'd watched the foursome of good-looking men snare the ladies' attention for a number of years.

''Jess, I'll be here until Monday. Can we put off our talk until later?'' Alex asked.

Jessica risked a look in Cal's direction, noting his fierce concentration on the three of them. ''Uh, I suppose, if you want to waste time on four testosterone-filled men.''

''Hey, don't prejudice the woman before she gets to know me,'' Tuck protested. Then he pulled out Alex's chair for her. ''Right this way, ladies.''

Jessica waved to Nita to load their nachos and drinks onto her tray and transfer them to the other table. She could've carried them herself, but the way her fingers were trembling, she feared she'd drop them in Cal's lap if she got within three feet of him.

As it was, she intended to stay on the other side of the table.

THE MINUTE Cal realized the ladies were heading in their direction, with Tuck riding herd, he leaped to his feet and grabbed two chairs from a nearby table.

The other two guys stood, also, and scooted chairs around to make room.

Cal abandoned the chairs to step forward. It wasn't the blonde he wanted to meet. He wanted to be sure he had Jessica at his side. Somehow he suspected she'd try to avoid him.

"Tuck invited us to join you," Jessica announced in a rather breathy voice, unlike her usual mellow tones.

Spence and Mac assured her of their welcome, as if there'd been any doubt. Cal kept quiet but snaked out a hand to snag Jessica. "Right here, darlin'," he said softly.

"Uh, no, I—"

He tugged lightly but firmly, his gaze steady on her face. Her cheeks reddened, but she capitulated, sitting beside him.

After the blonde was seated, Tuck made the introductions. "These guys are Spence, Cal, and Mac. But you won't be interested in them when I'm around." He slid his arm along the back of Alex's chair and grinned at her.

"Oh, really? It's too bad you're so modest, Tuck, since I really go for guys who have a lot of self-confidence.'' Then she shifted around in her chair until she almost had her back to him and looked at Spence.

''Are you all cowboys, too?''

While Spence was explaining their occupations, Cal leaned closer to Jessica and whispered in her ear, ''We need to talk.''

She didn't turn toward him. ''I'm in the phone directory.''

Damn it, he knew that! He didn't call her often because…well, because it was dangerous. That thought stopped him. What was he talking about? Jess was an old friend, almost a member of his family.

''I mean, about you dating Johnny. That's not—''

Alex, not realizing Jessica was having a private conversation, interrupted. ''Jessica, how have you managed to hide these handsome guys away? If you ever brought them to Dallas, they'd be eaten alive.''

''But we'd die happy,'' Tuck assured her.

Jessica rolled her eyes. ''Actually, Mac and Cal have lived in Dallas.''

''Really? When? Did you like it?''

Cal was forced to respond to the woman's questions out of politeness, but he didn't want to. Mac, in addition to answering her questions, asked a few of his own, which got Cal's attention, however.

''What are you doing in Cactus? We're not exactly on the way to a big city.''

''I'm here to help Jessica with the sale,'' Alex said. ''I'm her attorney.''

''What sale?'' Cal demanded, startled.

"Oops, sorry, Jessica," Alex hurriedly apologized. "I assumed your friends knew."

"It doesn't matter," Jessica assured her. "They would hear about it sooner or later."

"You still haven't explained," Cal said.

"I've been offered a substantial amount for my restaurants, and I'm thinking about taking the offer."

Cal frowned. He knew Jessica had opened several other versions of The Old Cantina in nearby towns, but he didn't think three restaurants would draw a major buyer. "Who's interested in three measly restaurants these days?"

"'Three measly restaurants'?" Jessica repeated, her voice rising. "I'll have you know, Cal Baxter, I have nine restaurants and they're all quite profitable!"

"Calm down, baby," he said, putting a soothing hand on her shoulder. "I meant no offense. I guess I haven't been paying attention lately. I had no idea you'd opened up that many places."

"Don't call me 'baby'," she muttered. But at least she hadn't shoved his hand off her shoulder. He loved the smooth warmth of her skin. His fingers itched to pull her closer, feel her against him as he had a few minutes ago.

"Damn," he muttered under his breath. What was he thinking? This was Jessica! Maybe he was the one who needed more of a social life, instead of Jessica.

"Aren't you going to kiss him again?" Tuck asked. "I thought that was his punishment for calling you 'baby'."

Mac and Spence chastised Tuck for trying to stir up trouble. Cal, however, concentrated on Jessica.

Her cheeks were red-hot and she refused to look at him. He relived that earlier moment when her soft lips had pressed against his, her body had lined up against him, and his temperature had shot through the roof.

Tuck wasn't through being difficult. "Need another beer, Cal? You look a little warm."

Cal struggled to maintain his cool. "Nah, I think I'll switch to iced tea." He waved to Nita as she was going by. "Iced tea, please, Nita. And I think we're ready to order."

"I haven't even read the menu," Alex protested. "What should I order?"

Her question distracted Tuck from his teasing. Cal, knowing what he would order, since it was always the same, beef fajitas, leaned back in his chair. But he didn't remove his hand from Jessica's shoulder. He wasn't ready to do that.

Which meant he had a lot to think about.

JESSICA REMAINED TENSE the rest of the meal, and to her it seemed to go on forever. Cal never let her forget he was beside her. He kept his arm around the back of her chair, just barely touching her, and if she leaned forward, his big hand cupped her shoulder and pulled her back.

The man was driving her crazy. Over the last few years she'd managed to avoid him; she'd had to— out of fear that she couldn't control her desires, even if she could control her actions.

And she'd been successful—until today.

Cal and the restaurants. The two passions in her life. She'd never achieved her goal with Cal. Now she was thinking of selling her restaurants. What would she have left? A chill rushed through her.

"You okay? Are you cold?" Cal asked, leaning to whisper in her ear.

More shivers seized her. "No, I'm fine."

"But you're—"

"I'm fine," she repeated, flashing him a stubborn look.

As if she'd offered encouragement, he switched back to his earlier request. "When are we going to talk? Tomorrow? You want to come to the ranch after church?"

"Alex will be here all weekend. As her hostess, I can't abandon—"

He ignored her. "Say, Ms. Logan..." he began.

"Make it Alex," the blonde responded with a charming smile.

He returned her smile out of habit. "I bet Tuck would be willing to give you a tour of his ranch tomorrow after church, if you'd like. He has a fine operation."

He almost chuckled aloud as Tuck sent him a look of gratitude. No need to tell his friend that he was using him. Tuck was happy.

Alex glanced Tuck's way. "Would it inconvenience you? I'd really like to see a working ranch."

"I think I could squeeze in a tour. I don't work much on Sundays."

"Is that okay with you, Jessica? Can we tour the ranch?" Alex asked her hostess.

Cal held his breath, waiting for Jess to answer. He knew she wanted to avoid him, though he didn't know why.

Finally she said, ''I'll take you out there and leave you with Tuck, if you want. I have an errand to run.''

The various participants finalized the plans and Cal leaned closer to Jessica. ''I'll be waiting for you.''

Jessica gave a brief nod but didn't look his way.

She didn't want anyone to know they would spend that time together. As if they'd do something everyone couldn't see. Like make love.

She chastised herself for such ridiculous thoughts. All they did was make her want the big galoot more. And she was already beside herself with her futile dreams.

Years ago she'd made the decision to give up that particular dream, to move on, but every time she saw Cal, she had to fight that battle all over again. With a sigh, she began marshaling her arguments to convince herself his six-foot-three frame, wrapped in muscle that would have most women drooling, was nothing special. His gray eyes that turned to silver when he was moved didn't invade her dreams.

Most of all, his caring, his tenderness, his concern for her wasn't important. She could live without Cal in her life.

Yeah, right.

And his stubbornness didn't drive her crazy.

It had turned dark while they'd eaten. When they all left the restaurant, the men escorted the women to their cars. Not that there was any danger, but it was the gentlemanly thing to do.

''I'm looking forward to tomorrow,'' Alex said softly as Tuck opened her car door for her.

"Me, too," he assured her, a cocky grin on his face.

Cal trailed Jessica to her car. "I'll be waiting," he said, his gaze fixed on her.

Again all she did was nod.

He seemed to want something more, but Jessica slipped into her car. She'd already given him more than she should.

"I THINK you're getting a head start on us," Edith Hauk protested that night, arranging her cards.

The other three ladies at the bridge table looked up.

"Who are you talking to?" Ruth Langford demanded. "And a head start at what?"

Edith folded her cards against her chest and looked at Mabel Baxter with accusation in her eyes. "I'm talking about Mabel. I think she must've told Cal."

"Told him what?" Florence Gibbons asked, seemingly disinterested in Edith's complaint.

"About our bet."

Ruth immediately laid her cards facedown on the table. "Wait a minute. No one said we had to keep it a secret."

"You told?" Mabel asked.

"Well, I—I wanted to encourage Tuck."

"How much did you offer him?" Florence demanded.

"I didn't offer him any money!" Ruth returned, outraged by the accusation.

"You offered him something," Florence insisted. "I heard it in your voice."

"That's none of your business," Ruth said, raising her chin.

"I thought it was Mabel," Edith added, distracting everyone from Ruth's betrayal.

"Why would you think it was me? I haven't even seen Cal this week. He only drops by every now and then."

"'Cause he was the one kissing in public today," Edith explained.

Mabel's eyes rounded. "Who was he kissing? I haven't heard of him even dating anyone recently."

"Jess."

"Jess?" Mabel shrieked. "Why, that's—perfect," she decided, a blissful smile settling on her face.

"Don't you think we're giving up, Mabel Baxter," Ruth asserted with force. "There's a big difference between kissing and making a baby!"

Mabel just smiled.

JESSICA SLIPPED into a back pew just as the music began. If she was in town, she always attended the church services, partly because she'd done so with her mother each Sunday. Also, because it made her feel a part of the community. Last, but not least, because Cal was always there.

Today he sat beside his parents, about halfway down the aisle.

He looked back, catching her gaze, and smiled, then motioned for her to join them. She shook her head and turned to the minister.

After the service ended, she quickly headed for the door. When she felt a hand touch her shoulder, she expected it to be Cal. Instead it was his mother, Mabel.

"Jessica, I haven't seen you in a couple of weeks. Is everything going okay?"

Mabel had always treated her like a daughter, and after Jessica's mother's death, Mabel had come regularly to the restaurant to have lunch with her.

Jessica kissed her cheek. "Everything's fine. I guess Cal told you I was thinking of selling my restaurants?"

"Why, no! I had no idea. Do you want to sell them? If you need money, I could—"

Jessica laughed. When she'd first started, Mabel had backed her financially, but she'd paid her back within a year. "Thanks, Mabel, but I don't need money. I've just expanded so much, that I never have any free time anymore. I thought I might try something else."

"What? Another restaurant?" Mabel took a deep breath and lowered her voice. "*I* think you should start a family."

Jessica's eyes widened. "I don't think—"

"You're twenty-seven, Jessica. It's time you had some babies."

"Don't you think I should find a husband first?" Jessica teased, knowing Mabel would react.

Mabel surprised her, however. Instead of becoming flustered, Mabel calmly said, "Oh, I think we've got that taken care of."

"What are you—"

"Ladies." Mabel's husband, Ed, interrupted them as he threw his arms around both of them. "I'm starving. Are you ready to go, Mabel? Jessica, are you joining us?"

Jessica kissed his cheek, too. Never having had a father, she was particularly grateful for Ed's kindness. "No, I have a houseguest, Ed, but thanks for asking."

"You could bring your houseguest. Is it a woman? We're not talking about a man, are we?" Mabel asked, a frown on her face.

"She's a woman, but I've already started preparations for lunch."

"But we need to finish our discussion. I heard— That is, I think we have a candidate for—"

"Mom?"

It was Cal, who'd just walked over. "What are you talking about?"

Mabel raised her chin and stared at her only child. "Nothing that you need to know about."

Cal shifted his gaze to Jessica. "Secrets?"

"Don't look at me," she protested. "I don't know what Mabel is talking about."

"I'll come to lunch tomorrow, at one. Can you meet me?" Mabel asked Jessica. "I'll explain then."

"Of course. I'll look forward to it. Now I'd better get back to my friend." With a wave of her hand, she walked away, glad to escape an encounter with Cal.

"Wait, Jess."

Too late. She turned to find him directly behind her, having left his parents on the church steps. The shock of his presence caused her to stumble. Cal grabbed her shoulders to steady her, and his mere touch had her struggling to maintain an even tone when she spoke. "What is it, Cal?"

His hands slid down her arms to her hands.

"Don't forget you're coming to the ranch at one."

When his hands left hers and he turned away she felt cold and bereft. *As if I could...*

Chapter Three

Cal paced the floor, checking his watch. It was almost one-thirty. Where was Jess?

The sound of a car engine had him racing to the front window. He hurried to the door and watched her get out. Her long legs were clad in jeans and she wore a green sweater that almost matched the color of her eyes. She'd pulled her raven-colored hair into one long braid that reached her waist.

During their childhood, he'd taken scissors and cut her hair. Both mothers had been horrified and he'd been punished. Now he understood their reaction. He thought he'd take a knife to anyone who dared to cut that glorious hair.

"'Bout time," he muttered in greeting.

"Sorry. I didn't realize you were on a tight schedule. We can talk another time if—"

"Trying to avoid me?"

"Why would I do that?" she challenged.

"I can't think of any reason, but I'm getting the impression that's what you're doing."

She walked past him without responding.

As she was about to sit on the flowered sofa in the

living room, he motioned toward the door beyond the dining room table. "Let's go to the kitchen. We'll be more comfortable there."

The kitchen had been their playroom. That, or the backyard on pretty days. Rosa, Jessica's mother, hadn't wanted them messing up her handiwork, so she'd made them stay in the kitchen or outside until she'd finished cleaning.

"Have a seat," he said, pouring two cups of coffee from the pot on the cabinet. "I even have your favorite cookies."

He'd always teased her about her sweet tooth, though her love of desserts didn't seem to affect her slender figure. She had curves in all the right places without any excess weight. Which, he was certain, had no doubt encouraged Johnny to hang around her.

"Let's talk about Johnny," he growled as he joined her at the table.

"Let's not," she replied, a cool smile on her lips.

"Why not?"

"Because my social life is none of your concern."

He wanted to grab her and shake her until she changed her attitude. Didn't she know the dangers lurking out there for innocent young women? They didn't have much violence in Cactus, but he'd seen more than he ever wanted to.

"Jess, I'm only thinking of your safety."

"And you do such a good job of it that half the men in the county are afraid to even speak to me."

He didn't see anything wrong with that. "Good."

"So you want me to grow old alone? To never have children? To never love anyone?"

"No! Hell, no. I want you to be happy!" Cal roared.

Jessica knew that. She'd been under Cal's protective umbrella since she was little. But her needs had changed over the years—and Cal's protection hadn't.

She'd vowed to give up on Cal and get on with her life. But it was so difficult. She got up from the table and crossed the room to stare out the back door.

"Let's go for a ride," Cal abruptly suggested.

She was feeling closed in right now. It might be easier to talk to him on horseback. She turned to him. "Okay."

He led the way to the barn. "You remember when I first taught you to ride?"

Of course she did. Her life had changed when Cal had become a part of it. "Yes. You were a stern taskmaster...but good."

"I didn't want you to get hurt. As it was, your mother almost killed me when she found out."

Not that her mother had been able to stop Cal. But she'd come to trust him. Several times when Jessica had pushed the limits as a teenager, her mother had consulted Cal before she'd made her decision.

Which had frustrated Jessica.

"Remember when she was worried about me going to the drive-in movie with Larry? She called you and you arrived with a giant flashlight. I've never heard such terrible language as you shone that spotlight on a lot of couples in a clench."

Cal laughed. "I learned a lot that night."

"Well, I didn't. Larry was too afraid of you to even hold my hand, much less give me my first kiss." Cal had been dating a pretty girl his own age, and Jessica had seen him kiss her and been filled with jealousy. The only thing she could think to do was to find someone to teach her what Cal had already known.

"A good thing, too. You were too young to go to a drive-in movie."

She sighed in disgust. "You think I'm still too young to go."

He smirked. "Don't have to worry about it. The drive-in closed seven years ago." Then he sobered. "Your mother was a fine woman. She was right to call me."

"You just say that because she usually agreed with you," Jessica returned with a smile, fighting the unexpected tears. Though her mother had cleaned houses for a living and the Baxters were wealthy oil people, he and his parents had always shown her mother respect.

"That's because I'm always right," he informed her with a chuckle.

He lifted down the saddle she always used, along with the saddle blanket and bridle. "Can you carry these?"

"Don't I always?" she demanded. He had taught her well about the care of the equipment and the animal she rode.

He slung his own gear over his shoulder and they headed for the nearby pasture where the horses were grazing. Cal gave a piercing whistle that drew his horse, a gelding named Olé, the cheer usually heard for bullfighters.

Jessica called softly to the sorrel mare Cal had dubbed hers ten years ago. She was simply named

Red. Even though it had almost been six months since Jessica had been to the ranch for a ride, Red responded to her voice.

"Hello, pretty lady. How are you?" Jessica crooned to her horse as she petted her.

"Guess she hasn't forgotten you," Cal said. "You've neglected her lately."

"I've been busy with the restaurants." *And avoiding you,* she thought. Even though Cal was sheriff, he lived on the small ranch his parents owned on the edge of town. Mabel and Ed were living in a nice house near the center of Cactus.

"So, if you sell the restaurants, you'll have more time for Red...and old friends?"

Jessica looked at him sharply. "Are you insinuating I've neglected *you?*"

"You haven't been around much lately."

Her chin rose. "As if you'd notice. You spend all your time with the guys."

He'd slung his saddle onto Olé and was fastening the cinch. Peering over the saddle at her, he said with a grin, "Careful who you say that to. Makes me sound like I like boys better than girls." He waggled his eyebrows at her.

She couldn't hold back a giggle. Cal always made her laugh, even when she didn't want to. "Not likely. You've been seen with too many women."

"Hey, not all that many. I prefer quality over quantity."

"Right. Quality describes Bunny Williams." The blond, buxom cheerleader had been Cal's steady his senior year in high school. Even though Jessica had only been fourteen, she'd been insanely jealous.

"Old Bunny. I'd forgotten about her." He rounded his horse to check Jess's saddling abilities. "Maybe Bunny fell into the quantity category. But a guy's got to sow his wild oats, you know."

Which brought them back to the topic of their discussion.

"When do I get to sow *my* wild oats?" she asked, her back to him as she finished the saddling. When he didn't respond, she turned to look at him.

Shock filled his gaze. "*Your* wild oats? Girls don't— I mean, nice girls don't do that."

Jessica rolled her eyes and then swung into the saddle. "And what century are you living in?"

"Jess, you're not— I mean, Johnny— Don't you dare!"

Unable to handle his reaction, Jessica dug her heels into Red's sides and was soon racing across the pasture, leaving Cal still in shock.

It didn't take him long to react, however. She heard Olé's thundering hooves closing in on her lead. Knowing he was catching up to her and approaching a closed gate, Jessica eased back on the reins, slowing Red to a sedate lope, then down to a walk.

Cal let Olé run until he reached her side before pulling on the reins. He said nothing, however. He'd stepped on too many land mines the past two days.

It wasn't that he didn't know things had changed. After all, he hadn't been alone when he'd sowed his wild oats. But he'd never thought of Jessica as a woman, someone who would— He shut down his thoughts. He couldn't go there.

"Jessie," he said in a low voice, "I didn't mean... You're still my little sister. I—"

"No!"

His brows soared. Had he misstepped again? He'd always thought of her as his little sister. *Not when she kissed you,* an irritating voice reminded him. He shook his head. He didn't want to go there, either.

"What do you mean, no?"

"I'm not your sister."

"Well, no, not technically, but—"

"I'm not your sister, technically or otherwise."

"I didn't mean we were blood-related, but I've always treated you like—"

"Don't I know it!"

"Why am I not getting to finish a sentence? What have I done that's so bad? Why am I in the doghouse?"

"Do you know how intimidating it is to date a woman the sheriff treats as his personal property?"

"Of course I do. That's how I knew you were safe. And I didn't treat you like personal property... I mean, it's not like I was dating you or anything. I just treated you like my little sister."

They'd reached the gate and she sat, solemn-faced, in the saddle as he leaned over to open it. They both rode through and then he refastened the latch.

"Heaven forbid you should ever become a daddy," she said with a resigned air.

"Hey! I'd make a great daddy!" he protested, becoming more and more confused by their conversation.

"You'd never let your little girl out of the house without an armored division to accompany her."

He grinned. "I'm not that bad. I'd only require a posse."

When the corners of her lips tilted up, he relaxed a little. He loved to see Jessica smile. Her low chuckle was a bonus.

With her response, he felt able to ask an important question. "Jess, what am I doing wrong? I've upset you, but I'm not sure how."

She pulled her mount to a halt and reached over to cup his cheek in her hand. "Oh, Cal."

He covered her hand with his and brought it to his lips for a kiss. "That doesn't tell me much."

She snatched her hand away and started Red moving again. She never seemed to want him to touch her anymore. After she came back from Texas Tech, he'd noticed a change in her, figured she was growing independent. He'd tried to back off. He'd moved to Dallas for a couple of years, and when he returned, there'd seemed to be a lot of space between them.

"Tell me what's wrong," he said as he caught up to her again.

"I can't."

"Why not? You used to tell me everything."

"Cal, we're not children anymore."

"I know that. I don't follow you around now."

"No, but you've warned the male population within fifty miles to stay away from me."

"That's it? You're not getting enough dates? I can fix you up with...let's see, Donald Hoskins. He's a nice guy."

"He's a nerd, big-time!"

"Well, there's Arnold Beatty."

"He's the postman."

"So? The mail is important."

"He's also divorced with two kids."

"You'd be a good mama," he assured her, watching her carefully.

She sighed as if the weight of the world was on her shoulders. "You don't understand."

"I understand that Johnny is the wrong man for you."

"Most women like to make that decision for themselves."

"I'm saving you the trouble," he assured her.

She rolled her eyes again. "Thanks but no thanks."

He shrugged his shoulders and remained silent. He knew his warnings wouldn't go away. As long as she stayed in Cactus, she'd be safe.

Except for Johnny.

Not that he was that bad a man. Johnny had gotten into some trouble as a juvenile, but he'd grown up. Now he sold used cars and was doing pretty well, from what Cal could tell. But there had been one incident of domestic violence with a girlfriend. And the man didn't accord Cal's warnings the respect Cal thought they deserved.

"Is it because he's not from one of the oil families?"

He frowned and reached over to pull her horse to a halt. "That's low, Jess, and you know it. Your mother didn't have oil money, and it never bothered either me or my parents."

"I know. But I don't see anything wrong with Johnny. We have something in common. We both grew up on the wrong side of the tracks, and we've both achieved our goals. What do you have against him?"

He's sniffing around you. He couldn't give that as an answer. "I've heard rumors about some wild parties. There's some police business I can't talk about. He's been carrying on with Lydia Deloach for a couple of years. Then he dumped her."

"Maybe she dumped him."

"Nope. She's been moping around town for a couple of months, telling everyone she talks to about how she loves Johnny."

Jessica turned away and tugged on her reins. Cal released his hold but nudged Olé to keep up with the other horse.

Jessica rode to the edge of Dry Creek, which flowed through Cal's property. It got its name because each summer it dried up to a small trickle. But now, in October, it was several feet deep with precious water.

She swung down from the saddle and Cal admired her lithe form, her elegant movement, her sexy rear. At that thought he shut his eyes and tried to erase the image.

But he couldn't. She did have a sexy butt. In fact, every inch of her radiated sexual attraction. That's why he had to work so hard at protecting her.

Any man who looked at her would immediately think of bedding her. Of unbraiding her black satin hair, spreading it across her bare shoulders, running his hands— Damn it! What was wrong with him today?

He swung out of the saddle, glad to move, hoping his jeans wouldn't be quite so tight if he managed to get his mind on something other than Jessica.

She knelt and dipped her hand into the clear water, her braid slipping over her shoulder.

"You thirsty? I've got a canteen on my saddle," Cal hurriedly said. As clean as the water looked, he never trusted the purity these days.

"No, I was just...a little warm. I thought I'd cool my face a little."

Cal stayed back, his mind working frantically for a way to convince Jessica to steer clear of Johnny. That was his goal for today.

"Listen, baby, some men get...physical with a woman when she doesn't do what he wants. I can't tell you anything specific, but—"

She stood up and swung around to stare at him. "Johnny? Are you saying—"

"No. I can't. But he's not someone you should be hanging around."

She stepped toward him, still staring at him. "So you're not warning me because you don't think I should have a social life. You're warning me because Johnny specifically is a problem?"

"Yeah." He didn't want to examine the relief that filled him when Jessica finally understood.

"Okay. I'll look for someone else. I thought... I mean, he understood how important it was for me to succeed. He didn't worry that I was more successful than him. Maybe I overlooked some things, but we've just gone out a couple of times, casual dates."

"What are you talking about? Why was it important for you to succeed? You mean, with the restaurants?" He hadn't ever considered the fact that Jessica might feel inferior. It couldn't be that. She was an incredibly beautiful woman, and she had the sweetest nature.

"Of course with the restaurants. With money. With my life. I wanted to be good enough for…for the Baxters," she said softly, giving him a rueful smile.

He grabbed her arms, pulling her against him. "What the hell are you talking about? You were always good enough for me. And for my parents!"

"But not for others. The prejudice has lessened now, for everyone, but I was a bastard, a half-breed, from the wrong side of town. I wanted to prove there was more to me than that."

"Baby, you are a beautiful, intelligent woman. No man would think—"

"Some did. I suffered less than some of the girls, because everyone knew you were my protector." A half smile flitted across her face. "So I guess I shouldn't be complaining about your protection. Darn it, I've lost my steam, Cal. I came out here determined to tell you to back off and here I am thanking you!"

He smiled at her. "Good."

She smiled in return, then turned serious. "You've been an important part of my life, Cal. But I don't want to grow old with no husband, no children. That's why I started dating Johnny. He was willing to go out with me."

"But you said you wouldn't keep on—"

"No, I won't. But that doesn't mean I'm going to join a nunnery, either." She pulled herself from his grasp and swung back into the saddle. Then she looked at him again. "Thanks for talking things out with me. And thanks for all the protection. But I'm a big girl now. It's time to let go.''

She waited for his response. But he didn't have anything to say. With a nod, he mounted and turned Olé back toward the barn, assuming she would accompany him.

Holding Red in check for a minute, she put some distance between them. After all, she didn't want him to hear her heart breaking.

JESSICA GOT TO the restaurant the next day after Mabel had settled at the table they always used. Mabel smiled at her as she sat. ''I hope this wasn't too inconvenient for you, dear.''

''No, of course not. I ran a little late because Alex and I were going over some papers,'' Jessica explained.

''Alex? A man?''

''No, don't you remember? I told you she was a woman, visiting from Dallas, helping me to decide about the sale of my restaurants.''

''Oh, yes. The name threw me.'' Mabel frowned, then looked up at Jessica. ''Are you going to sell the restaurants?''

Jessica sighed. ''I haven't made my final decision, but I'm leaning that way. My life has gotten too crazy lately, trying to handle all nine restaurants. I don't have time for a personal life.''

''And that's why we need to talk,'' Mabel insisted. ''It's time you focus on marrying and having babies.''

Jessica bit into her bottom lip. ''I'm afraid I don't have any real prospects for a husband, Mabel. Your son has made sure of that.'' There was Johnny, of course, but Cal had convinced her to drop the man. She hadn't heard about Lydia or about troubles with the police.

"Not true, dear," Mabel said firmly.

Jessica's eyes widened. Mabel had made just such a cryptic remark yesterday. "What are you saying, Mabel?"

"Cal."

Jessica stared at Mabel and then burst into laughter.

"Oh, please, Mabel, that's funny, but not an option."

"Why not? You love him, don't you?"

Mabel sat back in satisfaction while Jessica sought an answer. It wasn't easy. Jessica didn't want to lie.

"I'm fond of Cal, of course, but we're not...not that close."

"Close?" Mabel waved a hand to dismiss her response. "Nonsense. It's more than that. You're the daughter I never had. I love you and I want you to be the mother of my grandbaby."

"If I ever have children, Mabel, you know I'd want you to fulfill that role. I love you, too, but—"

"No, they have to be Cal's children."

"What are you talking about?"

Mabel twisted her napkin. She'd debated telling Jessica the truth. With a shrug of her shoulders, she said, "You see, we made a bet, 'cause we're all tired of not having any grandchildren."

"Who's 'we'?"

Mabel named her cohorts in crime. "It's because those boys all have each other. We need to get just one of them married. Then the others would do the same."

"A nice theory," Jessica said with a rueful smile, "but I don't think so."

"No," Mabel assured her. "Our plan will work. And I'm going to win. That Florence thinks she's got a plan, but mine is better."

"What is your plan?"

"It's simple. You seduce Cal."

"Mabel!" Jessica stared at her surrogate mother, horror in her eyes.

"Well, of course. I don't know why you haven't tried it before." Mabel frowned, a sudden thought striking her. "Are you a virgin, dear? Is that why you're so shocked?"

"No. I mean, I'm not— Cal isn't nearly as modern as you."

Mabel smiled. "Men never are, especially if we're talking about their women."

"I'm not Cal's woman."

"Of course you are, Jess, darling. And everyone in town knows that except Cal. Men are so dumb sometimes." She waved a finger toward Jessica. "So you have to get his attention."

"I can't do that," Jessica whispered.

Mabel gave her a superior smile. "I heard you already had." When Jessica looked as if she didn't understand, Mabel made sure she did. "You kissed him right here in this restaurant."

"A kiss is a lot different from…from what you said."

"I know. It will be much more effective. If you can, try to get pregnant."

Jessica stared at the woman she thought she knew, a kind, gentle woman, sedate, conservative. And she had recommended Jessica seduce her son and trap him into marriage with a baby.

She shook her head, her eyes wide. "That would be unfair, Mabel. I can't trap Cal. If he doesn't want—"

"Of course he does, sweetheart. He just doesn't know it. You're the perfect wife for him. And I love you dearly."

"Oh, Mabel," Jessica murmured, tears filling her eyes. "I can't imagine a more wonderful mother-in-law, but I can't seduce Cal."

"Hmm, I suspected as much." She reached over and patted Jessica's hand. "Don't worry, dear. I'll find a way. You just go along with whatever I figure out. We'll pull it off."

Jessica panicked. Who knew what Mabel would do. "No, Mabel, really, don't try—"

Mabel stood, waving a hand in Jessica's general direction, as if dismissing her concern.

"But wait, Mabel, we haven't eaten."

"Oh, dear girl, I don't have time for food. I have plans to make. Oh, it's going to be so wonderful when we're all really family."

With a big smile, she walked out of the restaurant, a determined look on her face.

Jessica stared after her, frantic thoughts racing through her head. What would Mabel do? And how would Cal respond?

An even better question was, what was Jessica going to do? She couldn't follow Mabel's suggestion.

Could she?

Chapter Four

Mabel didn't waste any time.

After consulting her calendar and giving her plan considerable thought, she called her son.

"This is Sheriff Baxter," Cal's deep voice proclaimed, all business.

"Yes, dear, I know. Do you have any plans for Friday night?"

"Hi, Mom. I don't know. Why?"

"Don't be cagey with me. I need you to come to our house that night. It's important."

"Why?"

"I'm throwing a surprise party for your father." She was glad he couldn't see her triumphant smile. He'd recognize she was lying. But she knew her son. He'd be there for his father.

"A surprise party? Will Dad like that? And what are you celebrating?"

"You father will be delighted. And I'm not telling you what it's for. It's a secret. Will you be here?" She held her breath. If her son couldn't make it, there would be no point to the party.

"Of course I'll be there. What time?"

"It will start at seven, but you should come a half hour early to help me."

Her next call was to The Old Cantina. "Is Jessica still there?"

"Yes, ma'am. One minute."

She repeated her request and received the same response. Suspicion. But, as she'd planned, Jessica, too, capitulated for Ed.

"But, Mabel, about what you said earlier, don't...don't try to trick Cal, okay?"

"Trick Cal? Why would I do that?" Her smile widened. "I've got to go, dear, but I'll see you Friday night. Oh, and Jessica, wear something sexy." She hung up even as Jessica gasped.

Next she called her co-conspirators. She felt so sure her son was going to marry Jessica, she could be big-hearted. Each of them was given carte blanche to invite every single woman they knew. That way Cal wouldn't suspect Jessica was his personal Waterloo.

He'd stay so busy keeping an eye on her, chasing the other men away from her, that he wouldn't even notice the other women.

SEVERAL TIMES during the week, Cal wondered about the party his mother was giving. He'd even tried to tease an answer out of her, but she deftly avoided his questions. Even without answers, he would be there for his father. He had been fortunate in his parents. In spite of being wealthy, they'd taught him solid values, encouraged him, and still tried to be there for him even though he was fully grown.

Unlike Jessica's parents.

Her mother had been wonderful, but her father had married someone else and left her mother stranded and pregnant. He'd explained to Jessica's mother that he couldn't marry a Mexican.

Jessica's mixed parentage had given her a startling beauty, with her dark hair and green eyes. But it had also given her pain.

Another reason Cal needed to protect her.

Though Friday was a busy day, he left the office in plenty of time to shower and change and arrive at six-thirty. His mother hadn't mentioned Jessica, but he knew she'd be invited. His father would want her there.

Anticipation filled him as he pulled into the driveway of their spacious, elegant house. Since he'd arrived early, there were no cars there yet.

"Mom?" he called as he came through the front door.

"Perfect, dear," she returned, walking from the kitchen into the foyer. "You're right on time. I need you to do me a favor. Can you go pick up Jessica? I don't want her driving home late by herself."

"Good thinking. Shall I go now? We'll be back before anyone arrives. Will Dad be suspicious?"

His mother gave him a merry smile, making him frown. "Not at all, dear. And Jessica can help me get ready."

"Okay."

As soon as Cal was out the door, Mabel moved to the telephone and dialed a number by memory. "Jessica? Cal just called and offered to pick you up on his way over here."

"That's not necessary, Mabel. I'll drive myself."

"Oh, dear, I'm sorry, but he's already left. Do you mind terribly much?"

"It's not that I mind, Mabel, but it's too much trouble for Cal. He might have plans for afterward."

"I'm sure he won't. But if you don't want to ride with him, I suppose you can tell him. Only, try not to hurt his feelings." She waited, her smile widening, as Jessica debated her answer.

"Mabel, I shouldn't go along with this, because I know what you're doing. But Cal doesn't, so I guess I'll accept a ride this time. But I'm telling Cal. So you'd better stop your shenanigans."

"Of course, dear. I'll see you in a few minutes."

Stop? She was only getting started.

JESSICA CHECKED HERSELF in the full-length mirror on her closet door. She'd told herself not to do as Mabel asked, but she had. Instead of her usual loose clothing and flowing skirts, she'd bought something new to wear.

A very short, very tight skirt. Red. And a white crinkle top that molded her figure and left her shoulders bare. Then, instead of her usual braid, she was wearing her waist-length hair unfettered. She sprayed a little extra perfume between her breasts and took a deep breath.

Maybe Mabel had a point.

She'd never pushed Cal. She'd always accepted his guardianship, even as it irritated her, and hoped he'd realize she cared for him on his own.

Until she'd kissed him on Saturday.

Even thinking about that few seconds left her

flushed...and wanting more. And tonight she was serving notice. If Cal didn't want her, maybe she'd attract someone else. It was time to get on with her life.

The doorbell rang.

After taking a deep breath and straightening her shoulders, she walked to her front door, only stopping to pick up her purse and keys on the way. She swung open the door, a nervous smile on her lips.

"You didn't check to see—" Already in the middle of his lecture, Cal's gaze slipped below Jessica's eyes and came to an abrupt halt. "Damn it, Jess, what are you doing?"

She pretended she didn't know what had caused his outburst. "Going to a party for your dad."

"I hope *he's* not the one you're planning to seduce," he growled.

She blinked, not expecting the attack. She'd hoped to see admiration. "I beg your pardon?"

Putting his hands around her waist, he picked her up, moved her back out of the doorway, and entered. Then he set her down. "You'd better hurry and change. Mom wants us there early."

She stared at him. "Change? Why would I do that?"

"Because what you're wearing is liable to incite riots. The men will all be trying to get close to you, and the women will want to pull your hair out."

"Don't you think you're exaggerating just a little bit? My outfit may be a little...flirtatious, but other women dress the same way all the time." She raised her chin, irritated by his response.

"You're really going to wear that outfit? Leave your hair loose?"

"What's wrong with my hair?"

"Hell, there's nothing wrong with it. But every man there will be thinking about running his fingers through it." His cheeks flushed and he looked away.

His response encouraged Jessica a little. "*Every* man?"

His head whipped around and he frowned at her. "That's what I said."

That answer suited her. She decided it was time to end the discussion before it got out of hand. "We'd better go if we don't want to be late." She walked past him out the door.

He was still frowning, but he stepped outside.

She'd intended to tell him about his mom's plan on the way over, but after his response to her clothing, she decided to await the return trip for her revelation. She could have a little fun first.

CAL COULD HARDLY KEEP his eyes on the road.

Jessica's skirt left a mile of tanned legs visible to his eyes. And that blouse was no better, baring her shoulders, dipping slightly between her breasts, letting a man's imagination work overtime.

"Where did you buy those clothes?"

"Why? You want to shop for your girlfriend?" she asked as if the idea didn't bother her.

He swallowed, his mouth dry. "No! But I don't think— I mean, it's not a good idea to dress so suggestively. Some men might get the wrong idea."

She gave a heavy sigh, as if disturbed. "But not you."

"What? Of course not! I know that you're not that kind of woman." He pressed his lips together, hoping to distract himself from the urge to trace hot kisses over those soft shoulders.

She rolled her eyes and looked out the truck window.

She'd been doing that a lot lately, as if he just didn't get it. Whatever *it* was.

They didn't have far to go, since Cactus was a small town. He couldn't think of anything else to say before he pulled into the driveway. "Look, I'll keep an eye on you tonight. If you get in trouble, give me a look."

"What kind of trouble do you think I'll get into?"

She couldn't be that naive. "You know what kind of trouble."

She leaned toward him. "You mean, someone might want to kiss me?"

Her soft red lips were only a couple of inches away. Did she know how much she tempted him? Maybe he should kiss her, let her know firsthand what he meant. No sooner had the thought crossed his mind than he acted on it.

He'd meant to kiss her gently, but hunger burgeoned like a sudden spring storm and he pulled her against him, his lips pressing hers, pleading for entry.

She opened to him at once, her arms stealing around his neck, her breasts pressing against his chest. He came up for air at some point, he wasn't sure how long, but slanted his lips over hers again. His hands slipped beneath the top of her blouse, eagerly seeking the soft breasts that tormented him.

Someone banged on the window of Cal's door, and they both jumped apart.

"Damn!" Cal muttered. He looked over his shoulder to discover Spence standing there, grinning. Cal opened his door and stepped out. "Forget what you saw."

"Is that an order from the sheriff?" Spence asked softly.

Cal didn't hesitate. "No, that's a request from a friend. That shouldn't have happened."

Spence smiled. "I'll forget it, but if you're not planning on advertising it to the world, you'd better remove that red lipstick from your face."

With a groan, Cal whipped a white handkerchief from his khakis and scrubbed his lips while he moved around the truck to open Jessica's door, to see if she was okay.

And still speaking to him.

"Baby, we'll just pretend that didn't happen. I wanted to show you what could happen, but it... Well, things got out of hand. I apologize."

She sat still, not looking at him. "You want to forget it happened?"

"Yeah. It was a warning, nothing else."

"A warning." Still she didn't move, nor look at him.

"Yeah. Are you going to get out?" He reached in to grab her around the waist and set her on the ground. After all, his truck was high up, and she'd revealed a lot of leg when she'd gotten in.

"Don't touch me!"

He frowned. "Are you mad at me?"

"No. But I can get out on my own."

She did, and though he enjoyed the way her skirt slipped up, he chastised himself for his appreciation. Clearing his throat, he added, ''Spence won't say anything.''

''Good.'' Without looking at him, she hurried to the front door of his parents' house.

What was wrong with her? He'd apologized. True, he'd gotten carried away, but Spence's arrival had taken care of that problem. If he hadn't arrived when he had, Cal knew he'd have pulled that blouse down and made love to her breasts until she'd cried for mercy.

The thought of what he'd wanted to do caused a reaction that he wouldn't be able to hide if he went in the house now. He took a deep breath and tried to think of other things, like changing the oil in his truck. He'd been needing to do that. Or calling the vet to discuss his bull. Old Toro didn't seem to be feeling good lately.

Probably had too many cows to service.

Damn! That didn't help. His mind immediately flew to Jessica. Tuck's comment about getting Jessica pregnant popped into his head. He closed his eyes, hoping inspiration would hit him to erase those pictures.

''You sleepwalking, Cal?'' Tuck called.

Cal was on the far side of his truck, with it between him and his friend. ''Trying to get rid of a headache.''

''Rough day?''

''So-so. Glad to see you. I assumed Mom would invite everyone, but since it's a party for Dad, I wasn't sure.''

Tuck grinned. "Yeah. Are you going in?"

"Sure. I was supposed to get here early, but I got…sidetracked. If I come in with you, I won't get in any trouble."

At least no more than he was already in.

"JESSICA, I expected you earlier," Mabel said as a greeting, her gaze roving Jessica's sexy outfit. "Perfect, dear, just perfect. You're— Oh, you need to fix your lipstick. It's a little smeared."

Jessica's cheeks burned. "I got a drink of water just before I left," she said hurriedly. "I'll go to the powder room and fix it."

And hope she could regain her composure before Cal came into the house. The man was driving her crazy. Kissing her that way to warn her? Any more warning and she'd have to go home and hide behind locked doors. Didn't the man have a clue? Did he think she responded to other men's kisses like that?

Oh, she'd tried. When she'd gone away to college, she'd already given up on Cal wanting her. She'd dated a lot of men. But after two dates, she'd always walked away. Only once had she tried having sex with a man. He'd been nice, sweet, very interested in her. When she'd agreed with his plea to become intimate, he'd been ecstatic.

She'd regretted her decision at once. But it was too late. And too late, she realized she was a one-man woman. And that one man was Cal. Either that or she was frigid. Now she knew for sure that she wasn't frigid. Not after Cal set her on fire in his truck.

After fixing her lipstick, she returned to the living

room, and was glad to see several guests had arrived. Florence Gibbons was there, as well as Spence's parents.

But there seemed to be an unusually high number of young women arriving. Jessica searched for Mabel, to see if she needed any help, of course, and also to ask her a few questions.

"Mabel, is there anything I need to do?" she asked when she found Mabel in the kitchen. After Mabel assured her she had everything under control, Jessica added, "I didn't know Ed was friends with so many young women."

"He'd better not be!" Mabel retorted with a smile. "I guess I can tell you now. The party is for Cal."

"Why?" Jessica didn't feel any better that all the young women had been invited for Cal.

"He just had his fourth anniversary as sheriff. I thought we should celebrate it."

"And you invited all those women because Cal is friends with them?" She was trying to be subtle, though she didn't think Mabel believed her.

"Heck, no! They're all camouflage." Mabel put her arm around Jessica. "You're the one. And dressed like that, you can't miss. Come on, let's make the big announcement."

Jessica stood to one side in the large living room as Mabel surprised her son. She figured Cal didn't have any idea about his mother's other surprise, either.

Jessica should have told him on the way over.

But she'd been distracted.

"Hey, Jess, you're lookin' fine tonight," someone said from behind her.

She turned toward the voice. "Johnny! I didn't know you were here," she murmured. Automatically her gaze sought out Cal.

He'd already spotted her and her companion, and his gray eyes were hard as steel.

"Yeah. Mrs. Baxter called and invited me personally. Nice of her, wasn't it?"

When she nodded, he leaned closer and wrapped his hand around her bare neck, whispering, "I'm glad she did. I wouldn't want to miss seeing you in this outfit. Maybe you can wear it for me when I take you out to dinner."

She didn't like his touch or the way he was practically hanging over her. "Maybe you should take Lydia out instead."

His gaze narrowed. "I don't want Lydia. I want you."

"Get away from her." Cal had suddenly appeared in front of them.

Jessica closed her eyes briefly, then placed a hand on Cal's chest. "Cal, please, we're just talking. Don't ruin your mother's party."

"I won't if he leaves you alone."

Johnny, who spent a lot of time building his muscles, couldn't compare to Cal who, at six foot three, topped him by five inches and fifty pounds of muscle.

"Listen, Sheriff," Johnny responded, refusing to give up, "you can't tell her what to do."

"No, but I can get rid of uninvited guests. After all, it's my party."

"Your mother invited me!"

Seeing a fight in her future, Jessica desperately sought a distraction. Music was her answer. "Dance with me, Cal. I want the privilege of the first dance with the honoree. If you'll excuse us, Johnny?'' She made it a question, but she was sure Johnny would recognize dismissal when he heard it. He might be a lot of things, but stupid wasn't one of them.

She wasn't sure Cal would accept her invitation. Sometimes men preferred fighting. To enhance her offer, she ran her arms up around his neck and leaned into him.

His big hands curled around her waist and he pulled her even closer against him, moving fluidly to the center of the floor where the rug had been rolled up. Several couples were already making use of the available space.

Now that she'd achieved her goal, Jessica tried to ease back from his hold, but his hands kept her pressed against him.

''I thought you wanted to dance,'' he murmured, his breath warm in her ear as he bent his head down to her.

''Yes, but if we dance like this, people will think we're…you know, a couple. And…and the other women will think you're taken. Your mother invited a lot of women here tonight so you would have a good time.''

''I'm having a good time.''

He spun her around, then pulled her back against him. ''In fact, I haven't had this good a time in years.''

She was having trouble breathing. ''I think you're trying to control your temper. When you calm down, you may regret what's happening here.''

And something was definitely happening. She

could feel his arousal through their clothing. Was Mabel's plan working? Could she trick Cal like that?

In spite of how she felt about him, she didn't want him to fall into a trap. She only wanted him if he wanted her, without tricks.

She nibbled on her bottom lip. Finally she muttered, ''Remind me to tell you something on the way home.'' Until then, she decided to enjoy herself.

Chapter Five

Cal wasn't happy with his mother's surprise. Nor was he happy that she'd invited Johnny Boyd. But he couldn't object to dancing with Jessica. It was pure pleasure.

And he could justify his dancing with her because Johnny kept hovering around her. Cal let her dance with his friends, Mac, Spence, and Tuck, but the rest of the dances he claimed for himself.

He enjoyed himself so much, in fact, that when friends began to leave as midnight approached, he was startled.

"You're leaving already?" he said.

"Hey, man, work starts at sunrise," Tuck reminded him. He had his arms around two young ladies, but he didn't seem eager to extend his evening.

Cal nodded. After his friend walked away, he leaned down to Jessica. "Do you think he's interested in either of those ladies?"

With a sigh, she shook her head no.

Since she only confirmed his thoughts, he didn't question her answer. "Are you ready to go home?"

"Yes. Tuck's right, it's late. I can catch a ride with someone so you won't have to—"

"I'll see you home," he insisted, not wanting to end the evening. He knew Jessica considered him to be her big brother, and had no interest in him, but he intended to keep an eye on her.

"I have to help Mabel clean up," she murmured, her gaze searching the crowd for his mother. When she spotted her with her three friends, she left Cal's side and headed toward Mabel.

Cal watched as Jessica kissed Mabel's cheek, bringing a smile to his mother's face. In fact, he was relaxed, leaning against a wall, watching, when Johnny moved in on Jessica. Immediately, he straightened from the wall and hurried to Jessica's side, sliding his arm around her narrow waist, shifting her hip against his.

"You leaving, Johnny?" he said, nodding at his mother and her friends at the same time.

"Yeah. And I thought I'd offer Jessica a ride home," Johnny returned, frustration in his voice.

"Not necessary. She came with me."

"Man, when are you going to let her have a life? She's not some little lamb about to be attacked by a wolf." Johnny moved a little closer.

Cal retained his hold on Jessica. "I'm not stopping Jessica from doing anything she wants. Baby, you want to go with Johnny?" He was taking a gamble, but he didn't think Jessica would let him down.

"Thank you for the offer, Johnny, but I did come with Cal. I think Lydia needs a ride, though."

Cal breathed a sigh of relief after Johnny glared at Jessica before stomping away.

"Well, ladies, Jess and I are leaving. Mom, thanks for the surprise party. We'll see you around," he said, pulling Jessica toward the door.

He almost had her outside when Mac stopped them.

"Cal, you comin' tomorrow?"

Tomorrow? In spite of the fact that he'd been attending the informal rodeos in the spring and fall for several years, it took a minute for Cal to comprehend what Mac was asking. "Yeah, I'll be there, same as usual."

"Good. And we'll finish our day at The Old Cantina, okay, Jess?"

"Of course it's okay. My profits would dip considerably if you guys switched to the Dairy Queen for your Saturday nights," she said with a smile.

Mac kissed her on the cheek before he headed toward his hostess to say goodbye.

As they stepped outdoors, Spence joined them.

"Going home alone?" Cal asked, frowning. "There were a lot of ladies here tonight."

"Yeah, and most of them are in love with you," Spence returned, a grin on his face.

"Not likely, Spence. See you tomorrow?"

"Sure." He leaned over to kiss Jessica's cheek. "And we'll see you tomorrow afternoon," he added.

She smiled and nodded.

After Cal joined her in the cab of his pickup, he complained. "My friends are awful free and easy with their kisses."

"Surely you're not complaining about that, too?" she asked, laughing. "Next thing I know you'll want to lock me in a glass case."

"Not wearing those clothes. I think you'd better burn them after you get home."

She frowned at him. "You really don't like them?"

"It's not a question of liking. Any man would like them, but they send the wrong kind of message."

He felt her stare and turned to meet her gaze. Instead of compliance, she raised her eyebrows and murmured, "I think I should buy some more just like them."

"What?" he roared. "You can't mean that."

"Cal, I'm twenty-seven, soon to be twenty-eight. I want to marry and have a family. Immaculate conception isn't likely, so I need to find a man." She turned and stared out the truck window.

Cal sat dumbfounded. She'd mentioned something about getting on with her life, but he hadn't really believed she meant to find a man. Another man in her life. "Maybe you need to give this idea some thought. You know, be sure you want to make these changes."

"I've thought. A long time. But it's hard to find a man who isn't intimidated by Cal Baxter, Sheriff."

"I said I'd set you up with some guys," he said, noting that he sounded defensive. But he didn't want everything to change. He didn't want Jessica belonging to some other man. Nor did he want his friends married. His world seemed to be spinning out of control.

"I think I have to make the choice myself, Cal," she whispered.

And risk making a big mistake, Cal thought. He'd

been called out to more than a few domestic disturbances in Cactus.

He sought desperately for something to distract Jessica. He didn't want her to tell him to get lost. "Say, what did you want to tell me on the way home?"

She stared at him, her eyes wide.

"Don't you remember? While we were dancing you said for me to remind you to tell me something."

"Uh, yes. It's about your mother."

When she said nothing else, Cal, after coming to a stop in her driveway, shut off his engine and turned to look at her. "Well?"

"Your mother has decided it's time for you to marry."

"That stupid bet," he muttered.

"You know?" she asked in surprise.

"Yeah, I know. Tuck's mom told him. Actually, I think she tried to bribe him," Cal said with a laugh. "Anyway, he told all of us. Don't worry. We're not going to cooperate." He grinned at Jessica, sure he'd relieved her anxiety. But she was still staring at him, her eyes wide. "What? Is there something else?"

She ran her tongue over her full lips, and his temperature rose as his gaze followed its movement.

"Uh, yes, there's more."

"What is it, baby?"

"Me."

He swallowed, his throat suddenly dry. "You? You mean, Mom is trying to marry you off, too?"

She sank her teeth into her full bottom lip and he leaned closer.

"Don't worry, Jess, I'll tell her you're not ready."

Her chin rose. "But I am, Cal. The problem is that I think you should know she's trying to marry you to me."

"You? Me? That's ridiculous!"

She turned away, staring out the passenger window again.

Cal felt nausea rise in his stomach. "Listen, baby, I'll talk to her. She'll understand. And…and I'll help you look for a good man. I'll take care of everything."

Of course he would. He'd promised Jessica's mother as she lay dying that he'd take care of Jessica. He loved taking care of Jessica. So why did he feel as if he was about to lose his supper?

She turned to face him again, her look grim. "You do that, Cal Baxter! You take care of everything!" Then she yanked open the door and ran to her front door.

He opened his door to go after her, but by the time his boots hit the ground, she'd already entered the house and slammed the door behind her.

Something was wrong.

After an enjoyable evening, Jessica was angry with him, and he didn't know why. His mother was messing up, if Jessica was to be believed, trying to force Jessica to marry him. And he was feeling worse than he had when that old bull kicked him in the shin two years ago.

What should he do now?

JESSICA'S MOOD hadn't improved when she got up the next morning.

"It's your own fault," she muttered over a steaming cup of coffee.

She'd actually believed Mabel when she'd told her to seduce Cal and everything would be all right. Dancing in his arms, her body plastered to his, all evening, she'd begun to believe he might have finally realized how perfect they were for each other.

For three hours she'd been living in a fool's paradise. Until the drive home, when he promised to find her a man. What was he? Chopped liver?

No. He was an incredible man, sexy, tender, loving—but not interested in her.

It was about time she accepted what she'd known all along. He thought of her as his little sister and that wasn't going to change.

The phone rang.

"Jess? Wasn't last night perfect?" Mabel crooned as soon as Jessica answered.

"It was a nice party, Mabel," she replied, struggling to keep her voice even.

"Party? Who cares about the party? I'm talking about you and Cal. Those clothes were perfect. He couldn't keep his hands off of you."

"Mabel, he was keeping me from Johnny, that's all. If you hadn't invited Johnny, he wouldn't have danced with me at all."

Silence.

"But he kissed you before you came in."

"Yes, but— I don't know why, but I think he was trying to show me what could happen if I tempted a man."

"He thinks you don't know? At twenty-seven?

Lord have mercy, the boy is dumber than I thought he was!'' Mabel rasped, irritation filling her voice.

Jessica gave a watery chuckle. ''It's okay, Mabel. At least I've finally accepted that he doesn't want me.'' She swallowed back tears. She wasn't going to lose control. She'd had other bad things happen in her life and had learned to move on.

''Well, I haven't! I've just begun my campaign. Now, you're going to need some more sexy clothes, something that shows off your figure. Where did you buy those?''

Jessica thought about arguing with her, but in the end she gave up and told her the name of the store. It was a large store in Lubbock, about fifty miles away.

It wasn't that Jessica believed Mabel could pull off her plans. But if she, Jessica, intended to marry and have children, she'd need to find a man somewhere. And sexy clothes seemed to catch their attention.

''Great. I'll pick you up in twenty minutes and we're heading for Lubbock. My treat.''

''I can pay for—''

''Of course you can. But this is my plan, so I'll pay. Besides, you're my daughter, sweetheart. At least in my heart. And eventually you're going to be my daughter by marriage.''

''Mabel—''

''Twenty minutes.'' She hung up the phone.

Jessica stood there, the phone in her hand and a small smile on her face. Cal and his mom were a lot alike. Big hearts and stubborn minds. She loved them both.

How was she going to survive without them?

CAL PERCHED on the top rail of the chute pen, preparing to settle onto the rambunctious bull. But his heart wasn't into the spirit of the occasion.

The more he thought about last night, and the way the evening ended, the more depressed he became. Jessica wanted to get married. Apparently to any man but him.

Not that he wanted to marry Jessica, he hurriedly assured himself, because marriage wasn't something he was ready for. And Jessica was like a sister.

"Ready, Cal?" Tuck asked.

He snapped his head up, staring at his friend. "Uh, yeah."

When he didn't move, Tuck asked, "What are you waiting for?"

He didn't know. Except that Jessica wasn't really his sister. He couldn't continue to believe that old standby after their kiss in his truck yesterday. Or their close dancing last night.

But she seemed intent on finding someone else.

"Come on, Cal," another cowboy called. "We can't hold this animal much longer."

Okay, he'd get this over with. If he could ride this bull, maybe he could convince Jessica that— What? She didn't want to marry? That she might be interested in him?

That thought distracted him completely. The bull barely got outside the gate before he dumped Cal on the soft dirt. To add insult to injury, he stepped over Cal and trotted to the other end of the arena.

Cal limped to the side of the corral.

"Man, I don't think you were focused," Mac said as he reached out a helping hand to pull Cal over the fence before the bull could take another run at him.

"Probably not. I'm not feeling so well."

"Something you ate?"

"I guess," Cal conceded, but he knew better. His sickness had come upon him last night as he'd promised to find a husband for Jessica.

"You don't need to be crawling on the back of another stupid bull if your head's somewhere else. Hey, Tuck!" Mac called. "Cal's through, and I don't want to break any bones today. How about you and Spence?"

"We're both finished. I'll tell Leroy we're headin' on in to The Old Cantina."

Mac frowned. "Tuck doesn't sound any more enthusiastic than you do. Maybe there's a virus going around."

Cal would like to blame his sickness on a virus, but he didn't think he could. But he also didn't want to examine why he didn't feel well. How could he explain his stupid conclusion about riding the bull?

Half an hour later, after washing the dust off their hands and faces, the foursome took their usual table at Jessica's restaurant in Cactus.

"A round of beers, darlin'," Tuck ordered as Nita reached their table. "And nachos."

"Surprise, surprise," she drawled, teasing since that was always their order on Saturdays.

Mac put his Stetson on the table and stared at his three friends. "What's going on here? Everyone seems a little strange today."

"Guess we partied too hard last night," Tuck offered.

"It's a cloudy day," Spence added. "No sunshine. Downright depressing."

"Yeah," was all Cal could come up with.

"That's it?" Mac demanded, his voice rising. "Tuck, I've seen you party till sunup and still put in a day's work. Spence, the sun is back out now. And, Cal? 'Yeah'? That's all you can say?"

"Who are you? The sunshine fairy?" Tuck growled.

Cal ignored Tuck's sarcasm. "It's this damned bet our mothers have made. It's upsetting everything."

"You just have to ignore them," Mac assured him. "I am."

"You don't understand," Cal protested, about to inform them of Jessica's involvement in the situation.

Spence, however, spoke up. "Say, Cal, if you're wanting to win for your mother, you sure had a lot of chances last night."

Panic filled Cal. Had anyone noticed how much he'd enjoyed dancing with Jessica? She'd kill him. "What do you mean?"

"There were several ladies there last night drooling over you." That fact didn't seem to make Spence happy.

And it did absolutely nothing for Cal. *He* wasn't looking for a wife. "It doesn't matter."

"Who are you talking about?" Tuck asked, one eyebrow rising.

"There were several, but Melanie Rule definitely had her eyes glued to Cal and Jessica. You remember her? She's the cute brunette who works at the drugstore. The entire time I danced with her, she watched you. And she'd didn't appear to be happy about it."

"Kind of like the three of you," Mac interjected. Then his eyes widened and he snapped his fingers. "That's it! You three are acting like you're lovesick!"

"No way!" Tuck shouted.

"Forget it," Spence snarled.

"You're crazy," Cal returned.

"I hope you're right. Women will mess you up faster than anything." It wasn't the first time Mac had warned them about women problems. He figured he knew best since he'd already tried marriage.

Cal took a deep breath. "Actually, my problem is woman-related, but not for me."

The other three stared at him, waiting for an explanation.

"It's Jessica."

The reaction wasn't what he expected.

"You mean, you and Jessica?" Spence demanded.

"Of course he does," Tuck added.

"You finally woke up?" Mac asked.

He glared at his friends. "No! I'm saying Jessica wants to get married!"

"That's the only wedding I'd dance happily at," Mac muttered. "Jess is terrific."

"Not me!" Cal shouted.

"Easy, there, or the sheriff will be arrested for disturbing the peace," Nita said, suddenly appearing at the table.

Everyone remained silent as she set the beers on the table. Then she put down the large platter of nachos they always ordered. "Anything else right now, boys?"

"Nope. We'll order later," Cal said, wanting her out of the way so he could discuss his problems with his friends. As soon as she left, he leaned forward. "Look, Jess has decided she needs to marry so she can have kids. Something about that maternal clock they're always writing about."

"So, volunteer. You'll have Jess, and your mom will be ecstatic," Tuck suggested.

"She doesn't want me! I'm like a brother to her!"

"She didn't look like your sister when she locked her lips on yours last Saturday," Spence remarked calmly, staring at Cal.

Cal knew he was thinking of last night, too, in the truck. But he'd promised not to say anything about that mistake.

"Or when she was dancing with you last night," Tuck added. "You know, I've never seen Jess dressed that way before."

"And you won't again," Cal answered. "I told her to burn those clothes. And...and I showed her what could happen if she went around dressed like that." He stared at Spence, wanting him to know the reason for that embrace in the truck. At least, the reason he'd come up with to explain his behavior. "She's not very experienced, you know."

"So, if she doesn't want you, what's the problem?" Mac asked.

"I've got to find her a husband," Cal replied, his voice filled with sadness.

"Can't she find one on her own?" Spence asked.

"The way she looked last night, I suspect she'd have a line all the way to the city limits if she tried."

"Of course she could. No man still breathing would turn her down. But she's special. She can't marry just anyone. I want her to be happy."

Silence fell as they all stared at each other.

"Don't look at me," Mac protested. "I'm not getting married again."

"I didn't mean…" Cal began, the pain he felt in his chest at the thought of one of his friends with Jessica making speech difficult.

"Hell, Cal, we love Jessica, but she's almost like a sister to us, too," Spence added.

Tuck nodded.

"So where do I find a good husband for her? And don't suggest Johnny."

"There's got to be some nice man who'll be a good husband. Though not as good as you, Cal," Mac added.

Cal glared at him again. "For someone who hates the idea of marriage, you sure are saying some stupid things today."

"I just think no one could love Jessica and care for her as well as you," Mac said softly, his gaze focused on Cal.

Cal hoped he kept the pain he was feeling out of his face. "She doesn't want me," he said gruffly. "You should've heard her when she told me about Mom."

"Your mother? What about your mother?" Tuck asked. "You mean, about the bet?"

"No. I mean about Mom trying to force Jessica to marry me. She's decided she'll win the contest if I marry Jessica. And Jess wasn't happy about it. I could tell.''

He could barely face his friends. They all looked sympathetically at him, as if they knew how he felt. He hoped they didn't.

With a sigh, he added, ''I promised to find her a husband. It's not going to be easy.''

Tuck, who was facing the door to the restaurant, appeared to choke. Then he said, ''I think maybe it just got easier.''

''What are you talking about?'' Cal demanded.

''You may have told Jess to burn those clothes from last night, but, buddy, what she's wearing today is going to set every man in town on fire.''

Cal whirled around to stare at Jessica as she crossed the room toward them, pausing to greet old customers.

He felt his temperature rising.

Chapter Six

Jessica knew the instant Cal saw her.

A flush crawled up from her chest, not stopping until her cheeks glowed like the one red light in Cactus. She'd told Mabel she wasn't sure she could pull off her "new look."

She hadn't looked in Cal's direction, too worried about what she'd see, so she was nearly thrown off balance when he grabbed her arm.

"What the hell are you doing?" he demanded in a guttural voice.

She looked at his features, harsh with anger, and shrank back. "Hi, Cal. How are you?"

"I was a damned sight better two minutes ago. Come with me."

As if she had a choice. Oh, she could've made a scene. She knew Cal wouldn't force her. But it was easier to go with him and get this confrontation over with.

They went through the swinging doors and Cal came to a halt, staring at the staff-filled kitchen.

Jessica almost giggled at his stunned expression. Did he think she did all the work herself? In nine restaurants? "My office," she muttered, and became the leader of their two-person parade.

The space was scarcely large enough to be called an office, but it offered privacy, at least. She closed the door behind him and then leaned against the wall. "Well?"

"What are you doing dressed like that?"

She let one eyebrow slip up. She was prepared this time. "Enjoying myself. Being feminine."

Cal's mouth gaped and he struggled to speak. Finally he managed to get out a few words. "That outfit's even worse than last night's!"

Jessica smiled. Mabel had expressed the same sentiments only in different terms, accompanied by a wicked smile. Jessica had told herself it wouldn't make a difference, but she'd also decided it wouldn't hurt to torture Cal.

"No, it's not!" The halter neckline of her dress framed her voluptuous figure, exposing her back and shoulders, the vee-shaped front dipping scandalously low. The lightweight floral-print material seemed to float when she walked. The skirt stopped about three inches above her knees.

"We're almost into winter," Cal roared. "You're going to catch pneumonia."

He pronounced his words with all the arrogance of a doctor, sure he had a direct line to God.

"Cal, it's only October and we're experiencing Indian summer. It's eighty-five degrees out, for goodness' sake."

"It could be a hundred and five and you'd still need to be covered up."

"If it's that cold, why are you sweating?"

He ran a finger around the neck of his T-shirt. "We're not talking about me."

"We're not talking about me, either. If you'll excuse me, I'm going to greet the rest of my customers."

"Jess, at least put on a sweater," he pleaded.

"This dress would look ridiculous with a sweater." She said it calmly, as if fashion chic was her only concern.

"You're right. It would look better under a raincoat," Cal said, his clenched jaw making his words come out tightly.

"Are you on that ridiculous kick about what a temptation I am?" She stared at him. "I'm not exactly Marilyn Monroe."

"Aw, baby," he said, his voice suddenly husky. "Marilyn Monroe couldn't hold a candle to you. You're the prettiest woman in Cactus." He lifted a hand to tuck a strand of hair behind her ear, hair she'd left loose again today to curl down her back.

She leaned a little closer, drawn by his touch. "Are you going to show me what could happen to a woman if she dresses too sexy?"

As if mesmerized by her gaze, he leaned toward her, pulling even closer, until only a breath separated their lips. "Yeah," he began softly, "I'll show—"

She didn't wait for him to complete his sentence. Her hands flattened on his hard chest and her lips met with his, her tongue darting into his mouth, eager to taste him again.

With a groan, he wrapped his arms around her, pulling her softness tightly against him, opening his mouth and joining her in her feast.

Excitement raced through Jessica as she surrendered herself to Cal. He was hers, she could feel it. At least for this moment. Her fingers slid under his T-shirt, stroking the hair-covered chest, wishing she could follow her hands with her lips.

Cal ground his manhood against her, letting her know how hot he'd become in thirty seconds, and one hand inched closer to her breast, his thumb coming daringly near the vee of her dress.

The knock on the door functioned like a pail of cold water thrown at Jessica. It took Cal a little longer to gain control.

"Yes?" she demanded, her voice breathy.

"You have a phone call," Nita said.

Jessica stared at the desk where a telephone sat. Had it rung and they'd both ignored it? She certainly hadn't heard it.

"Um, okay, I'll pick up in here."

Cal immediately backed away. Then, as she moved to the desk, he opened the door, intent on hurrying away.

"Cal, wait," Jessica called, not yet picking up the receiver.

"I apologize," he muttered, but he never looked at her. He just charged out of that small space as if a hundred demons were chasing him.

WHAT HAD COME OVER HIM? If they hadn't been interrupted, he'd have taken her right there, up against the door, like a wild animal. Jessica. His little Jessica.

Cal was thoroughly ashamed of himself. It had been a while since he'd been with a woman, he admitted, but he was older now. Not so randy.

Or at least that's what he'd thought. But if he couldn't be trusted with Jessica, who could he be trusted with? She'd already let him know his mother's scheming upset her.

Of course, her behavior hadn't been completely innocent, either. Dressing like that, kissing him. But she expected him to protect her. She was inexperienced. It wasn't her fault that he couldn't control himself.

She probably wanted to test her feminine wiles. He'd heard that young women did that. Especially if they'd been sheltered for a period of time. God knew he'd tried to shelter Jessica. So maybe he'd taught her a lesson today. Maybe she knew now not to play with fire.

And maybe he could put out the fire one more time.

In the men's room he splashed his face with cold water until he gained some semblance of control. Then he rejoined his friends.

"You get Jessica straightened out?" Tuck asked, a grin on his face.

"No. I think I'm going to have to accept her behavior until I find her a husband. She's real determined."

Tuck's smile faded.

Spence frowned at Cal. "You're sure she's not interested in you?"

"I'm sure. Now, let's make a list. What eligible men do we know?"

His three friends, after exchanging sad looks, leaned forward and put their minds to the topic. Soon they came up with five men. Good men. A banker, a rancher, the drugstore owner, a home builder, and, last but not least, the young minister who'd come to town last spring.

"I'm not sure about Tony." It was Spence who named the minister.

"What's wrong with him?" Cal asked.

"Nothing, really. But the way Jessica's dressing, he might not be interested."

Cal bristled. "She may be dressing a little suggestively, but he'll be interested. Believe me," he assured them, his cheeks flushing. Jessica could tempt a saint.

"Are you going to tell her now?" Mac asked, his gaze going past Cal to the young lady heading toward their table, her look apprehensive.

"Why?"

"'Cause here she comes."

Cal spun around to stare at Jessica. She didn't look happy. He understood. She was embarrassed about what had happened as much as he was. Of course she was. She wasn't used to a man's hunger.

It was up to him to make her feel at ease.

"Hi, baby. Was the phone call serious?"

"It was Alex. She wanted to set up a closing for the purchase of the restaurants." She didn't look at him.

"Well, hey, I have some good news," he assured her, pasting on a brilliant smile. He was able to hold it in place until she'd glanced at him and looked away again.

"What's that?"

"We've come up with some potential husbands for you."

Mac stood and pulled another chair over between him and Cal. When he gestured for Jessica to sit, she slipped into the seat he'd been occupying, leaving the chair beside Cal for Mac.

That hurt. She wouldn't even get that close to him. Was she afraid he'd grab her again? Here in public? He slid the list toward Jessica. "What do you think of these as potential husbands?"

She glared at him before picking up the paper. "They look fine," she said after a moment.

His heart took another bruising. He'd hoped she'd look at the names and refuse to consider any of them. In fact, he told himself she might not have such an aversion to him as he'd thought, if she wasn't interested in the five sterling citizens he'd listed.

"So..." He cleared his throat. "Which one would you like to start with?"

"Whoever's on top. I bought some more new clothes today, so I'm prepared to wow him." She leaned forward, drawing everyone's gaze to her breasts, and grabbed Cal's beer, taking a long drink.

Cal stared at her. She never drank beer. In fact, she never drank any alcohol. What was wrong with her?

"Want Nita to bring you one of your own?" Tuck asked, staring at her.

"No, thanks, but tell her to bring all of you another round, on the house. After all, you should be rewarded for finding some husband material for me." She stood, ignoring their stares. "I've got to go. Let me know when you've bribed the first one on the list to go out with me, Cal. I'll be ready." She gave him a devilish smile and walked away.

His face heated up as he remembered just how ready she'd been a few moments ago in her office. Damn! What was wrong with the girl?

Mac leaned toward Cal. "What happened when you and Jessica went to the kitchen?"

Cal whipped his head around to stare at his friend. "Huh?"

"What happened—"

"Nothing! Nothing. She got a phone call. We didn't really get a chance to talk." That was the truth. He'd been too busy kissing her.

"She sure is acting strange," Spence said softly, staring at Cal. "Like her feelings are hurt or something."

Or something. She was regretting his behavior, Cal felt sure. Maybe she'd started out teasing him, testing his control, but she'd discovered he didn't have any. He must've frightened her.

But she hadn't acted scared at the time. He supposed women could get as carried away with sex as men. Maybe.

"Are you sure you want to go ahead with this?" Spence asked, nodding at the paper Jessica had left on the table.

"Yeah, I'm sure. You heard her. She liked the list," Cal said. He had to marry her off to someone else, so he couldn't touch her. Otherwise he'd lose her as a friend.

And he'd have nothing.

JESSICA STARED at her purchases. When she'd returned from Lubbock with Mabel, she'd had such hopes. Once more she'd let Mabel convince her to try for Cal's heart.

Instead she'd reached his libido.

She took her purchases, wadded them into a ball and threw it into the back of her closet. So much for sexy dressing. She'd never thought women who dressed that way were smart, anyway. They were simply putting their bodies on the market.

What they got in return were bodies.

She wanted a heart.

Cal's heart.

With a sigh, she sank down onto her bed. She'd told herself she'd get on with her life.

Now she had a list of names. She'd go out with all of them, if Cal could convince them. And one of them would become her husband, the father of her children, her companion for the later years.

He just wouldn't be the love of her life.

MABEL HAD ASSUMED that Jessica would spend Saturday night with Cal. Dressed as she'd been, Jessica could have convinced a eunuch to spend the evening with her.

Preparing for church the next morning, she said to her husband, "Ed, you don't have any objections to Jessica, do you?"

Ed frowned at her, distracted from putting his belt through the pants loops. "Objections to Jessica? For what? I think she's terrific. I love her like you do."

"I thought so," Mabel said with a warm smile. "It will be so great when she and Cal marry."

Ed looked as if he'd been poleaxed. "Did I miss

something here? Who said they were getting married?''

"Me. I'm going to get them married and then I'll get a grandbaby. And I'll win the bet."

Ed stepped toward her. "Woman, don't mess with Cal's personal life."

Mabel smiled. He reminded her a lot of their courting days. He'd tried to boss her then, too. "Why, whatever do you mean, Edward Gene Baxter?"

"You know what I mean. Leave Cal alone."

"You don't want Cal and Jess to marry?"

"I think it would be great. As long as it's their idea and not yours."

Mabel blinked her eyes, wringing a few tears to affect Ed. "You know Cal is my only child, my pride and joy. I would never do anything to hurt him."

Since they'd lost several babies after Cal, early in her pregnancies, Ed responded as she'd known he would. His arms came around her and he pulled her against him. "Aw, sweetheart, I know that."

She rubbed her nose against his neck. "Hmm, you smell good. Maybe we should be late to church," she whispered, her lips emphasizing her invitation.

He gently swatted her backside. "Behave yourself, woman. I've got that activity planned for a leisurely afternoon. Wouldn't want to have to rush it, would we?"

"Why, Ed, I had no idea. I thought you'd be watching the Cowboys." Every Sunday, Ed watched his favorite football team.

"They're playing on Monday night."

"O-oh! Good for them," she said before she gave him a kiss of promise for his afternoon plans.

Later, in church, she searched for Jessica. She finally arrived late, dressed in an ultraconservative navy-blue suit, not the kelly-green, formfitting suit with the very short skirt that they'd purchased the day before.

As soon as the service was over, Mabel headed for Jessica. "What's wrong? Where's the green suit?"

"It's not working, Mabel. It only makes Cal work harder to find a husband for me. He's already prepared a list."

"He probably made that list before he saw you last evening. He did see you, didn't he?"

"Yes. And I think he made the list afterward."

"I can't believe he—"

"Hi, Mom. Jessica."

The subject of their discussion stood a couple of feet away.

Mabel stared first at her son's closed features and then Jessica's. She took a step toward him. "Aren't you going to give me a kiss?"

"Sure," he said, dropping a kiss on her cheek. His gaze slid to Jessica and then away. She was staring off into space, as if fascinated by the drifting clouds.

"Well, how about you both come home with us for dinner? I can make—"

"No, I can't!" Jessica protested, panic in her voice.

"Sorry, I have plans," Cal said at the same time. He took a deep breath, then added, "I've got to talk to Trevor Heywood about something."

Mabel looked at Jessica sharply as her cheeks flooded with color. Was Trevor one of the ones on the list?

Trying to act nonchalant, she said, "Oh? Are you planning on taking out a loan? Your father and I—"

"Don't worry, Mom. It's nothing like that. I've got to go. See you. Jess, I'll give you a call."

He didn't wait for an answer, and Jessica seemed relieved.

"Well! Is Trevor's name on the list?"

"Yes," Jessica muttered.

Mabel watched as tears filled the child's eyes. She wanted to hold her and promise that Cal wouldn't hurt her, but she couldn't. "Come eat with us, dear. It'll make you feel better." Ed would understand about canceling their plans, once she told him about Jessica's tears.

Jessica blinked her dark lashes several times and tried a smile. It wasn't very good, but it was better than the tears. "Thanks, Mabel, but I have some things to do this afternoon. I'm going to Dallas tomorrow to complete the sale of the restaurants."

"Oh, my. Do you need me to go with you?"

"No, I'll manage. Thank you for offering, though."

"All right, dear. But I haven't given up. I want you to know that."

Jessica didn't seem thrilled with her promise.

USUALLY CAL SHED the tailored pants and a dress shirt five minutes after getting home from church. Today, he'd kept them on.

Now he crawled out of his truck in front of a large brick home in the best neighborhood in town. Trevor Heywood certainly seemed to be a successful man.

That was important. Cal didn't want anyone marrying Jessica for her money.

He strode to the door, afraid to wait any longer, knowing he'd prefer getting in his truck and returning home.

Trevor himself answered the door.

"Cal? Come on in," he boomed, closing the door behind the two of them.

"Are you alone, Trevor? I need to talk to you."

Trevor's eyebrows rose. He was a pleasant-looking man, but his features were a little soft, round. His handshake was loose, flabby. He always made Cal think of Porky Pig, even though he wasn't really overweight and he still had hair. Some.

"I hope nothing's wrong. I mean, one of my customers isn't in trouble, is he?"

His customers. The man acted as though he owned the bank. Of course, his father did, so maybe he was justified in feeling that way.

"No, of course not. It's…it's personal."

"You got money troubles, Cal?" Trevor asked in surprise as he led the way into a large room expensively furnished with sofas and a big-screen TV.

"No! Not at all." He certainly didn't want anyone thinking he was broke, Cal thought.

"Ah." Trevor waved to one of the sofas. After Cal sat, he took a seat opposite him. "Then what's the problem?"

"No problem. I, uh, wondered if you've been dating anyone lately."

Trevor stared at him. "Dating?"

"I don't remember seeing you around town with a lady, and I—"

"Are you insinuating I'm gay?" Trevor asked, rage trembling in his voice.

"Hell, no! You're not, are you?"

"No, I am not! I date a very nice lady from Lubbock. One has to be careful with his social life when he's a banker," the man explained self-righteously.

Cal wanted to spit out the taste those words left in his mouth. But Jessica had said to go ahead. Even so, he had to force himself to continue.

"Look, I'm not handling this conversation right. What I'm trying to say is, do you have any interest in dating Jessica Hoya?"

Chapter Seven

Trevor stared at him, his mouth open.

Cal waited.

"Why?" A speculative look filled Trevor's beady eyes.

"What do you mean, why? Why wouldn't you?"

"Because you've always warned people away. Has something changed? Have you got her pregnant and you're looking for someone else to take the fall?"

Cal couldn't believe the man's response. He leaped to his feet, his fists clenched. "Stand up, you bastard, so I can knock you down!"

"Hey, you can't blame a guy for wondering. I heard she's going to make a lot of money on the sale of her restaurants. Is she looking for some preferential treatment? How much? I might be interested in her if she's—"

Cal couldn't take any more. He walked out of the house as the man continued to speculate on Jessica's financial worth.

After roaring through town, he turned back and

went to the house Mac shared with his aunt. He needed help.

Ringing the doorbell, he waited for Florence Gibbons to come to the door.

"Why, Cal, come on in. What are you doing here?"

"I need to talk to Mac. Is he in?"

"Sure. He's stretched out on the couch watching football, like most every other man in town."

Mac looked up in surprise when he saw his friend. Standing, he shook Cal's hand and offered him a seat.

"Uh, I need to talk to you, Mac, but I don't want to interrupt the game."

"These aren't teams I care about. Dallas doesn't play until tomorrow night. How about something to drink?"

"Maybe a soda," Cal said, his gaze slipping to Florence. He couldn't talk in front of Mac's aunt.

"I'll get you a couple of them," Florence offered. "Then I'm going upstairs to read. It beats football anyday," she assured them with a grin.

As soon as Florence left the room, Cal said, "Mac, I'm in trouble."

"What kind?"

His friend leaned forward, a frown on his face, clearly taking Cal's words seriously. Which made Cal feel a little better. "It's that list we made."

Florence came back into the room with two glasses of soda and a basket of chips from The Old Cantina. "I hope when Jess sells those restaurants they keep making these chips. They're my favorites. That girl is a real businesswoman, isn't she?"

"Yeah," both men agreed, but they said nothing else to prolong the conversation.

As soon as Florence disappeared again, Mac asked, "What happened? Did you approach one of them?"

"Yeah. I started with Trevor Heywood."

Mac grimaced. "Never particularly cared for him. Do you remember in sixth grade when he got in a fight with a girl? And she won!"

Cal laughed. "Yeah. Well, we're crossing him off the list. I asked him if he wanted to go out with Jessica, and he asked if I'd gotten her pregnant and wanted him to take the fall." Cal grew angry all over again.

Mac muttered his opinion under his breath, a hurried look over his shoulder to be sure his aunt wasn't in hearing range.

"Yeah," Cal agreed. "My thoughts exactly."

"Okay. So, we still have four candidates, right?"

Cal nodded. "What bothers me, though, is I think I'm going about it the wrong way. I mean, Jessica is bright and beautiful. A success in every sense of the word. Why would a man hesitate?"

"How did you bring up the subject with Trevor?" Mac asked, studying his friend.

"Bring up the subject?" Cal asked, confusion in his voice. "I just asked if he wanted to go out with her."

"Hmm. I think we need more strategy. Let me call Tuck and Spence. We're going to have to do some planning before we run out of guys to approach."

An hour later the four men were gathered at the game table at one end of the den with a sheet of paper in front of them. Various ideas had been discussed, but nothing satisfactory had popped into their heads.

"I got it!" Tuck exclaimed.

"Well, it better be an improvement over your last idea," Cal muttered. Tuck had decided they should mail out announcements that Jessica was "uninvolved and looking."

"It is. I've cut down a lot of mesquite trees, and I'm going to burn them."

Spence frowned. "So what? We do that every year."

"Yeah, but if we call it a celebration of Jessica's sale of her restaurants, use the fire to cook a lot of steaks, and invite all the candidates, we can encourage them to, uh, hang around with Jess. Then it will seem natural-like."

Cal looked at all three of his friends, studying their reactions while he thought about Tuck's idea. Then he smiled. "You know, Tuck, I think you've got something there." He wrote down the idea on the paper. "It'll be casual, fun and innocent. No one will suspect."

"And we can invite Alex to the celebration, to make everyone believe that's the only reason," Tuck added, his gaze twinkling with excitement.

"We'll have to invite a lot of other people, too," Spence said. "Like at your party, Cal. Just so no one will suspect."

"Of course. Mom will help us," Cal said. "Especially when I tell her it's for Jess."

Tuck grinned. "I suspect all our mothers will pitch in since they're so anxious for us to marry. It might be best not to tell them we're trying to marry off Jessica. Let them think we're getting into the spirit of the competition.''

TUESDAY NIGHT, Florence Gibbons brought up the subject of the cookout.

''Anyone have any idea what's going on? It's not like these boys to plan a social event.''

''It's at Tuck's place,'' Edith Hauk reminded them. ''I assumed it was his idea.''

Ruth Langford, Tuck's mother, looked guardedly at her friends. ''I don't know. He's not talking to me, other than to ask that I help with the food.''

''I'm helping with the steaks,'' Florence said.

''I'm in charge of desserts,'' Mabel said with a serene smile.

Florence eyed her friend closely. ''I think you know more than you're saying.''

''The party is to celebrate Jessica's sale of her restaurants. Didn't they tell you?''

''Yes,'' Ruth admitted. ''But Tuck's all excited-like, as if he has plans. Not like that party at your house, Mabel. Even though he left with two women, I knew he wasn't interested.''

Florence's brow lifted. ''You mean he's interested in someone now? Who's invited?''

''Everyone from the invitation list of my party, plus any other singles in town, and, of course, Jess's attorney, that pretty blond lady.''

Edith frowned. ''Even Spence seems more interested. Lately, he'd been a little quiet. I've been worried about him. But with this party in the works, he's perked up a little.''

They picked up their cards and arranged them, the conversation languishing. Then Mabel asked, after bidding one diamond, "How's your plan coming along, Florence?"

Her friend glared at her. "Not well. I can't stir up any interest in Mac for remarrying."

Mabel smiled but kept her gaze on her cards.

"Mabel? Mabel Baxter, what are you thinking?" Florence demanded.

"I'm thinking I'm going to win," she said demurely. Then she smiled at her three friends. "At bridge, of course."

The other three groaned.

IT WAS TUCK WHO'D CALLED Jessica to tell her about the celebration they were planning. She'd been reluctant to agree to the party.

Truth to tell, she wasn't feeling too happy about her decision. The sale had brought her millions, which properly invested, would provide for the rest of her life. She should've been over the stars. Instead, she felt useless.

Alex had counseled her to take some time to decide what she wanted to do with her life. She was still young. She could start another business, travel, take classes at university.

Or stay home and be lonesome.

So far she'd opted for the last choice.

She stared at the television, watching another mindless sitcom. The doorbell surprised her.

She opened the front door to Cal.

She hadn't seen him since Sunday after church when he'd indicated he was going to start working on finding her a husband. Was he here to tell her he'd succeeded?

"Hi, baby. Can I come in for a minute?"

"Of course." She stood back, allowing room for his big frame to pass, then followed him in to where she'd been watching television. He settled on the sofa and she took the big chair next to it. It was safer than sitting beside him.

"What's up?"

"I thought I'd better tell you— Are you okay? You seem a little sad."

She pressed her lips together and looked away. Finally she said, "It's hard to adjust to the sale. I don't have anything to do."

He awkwardly patted her shoulder. "I guess it's a big change for you. You've been running in every direction the last few years."

She nodded, blinking back tears. Sympathy from Cal unmanned her.

"That's okay. We've got plans for you."

"Who is 'we'?"

"Mac, Spence, and Tuck are helping me."

"Do what?"

"Find you a husband. Don't you remember? We talked about it on Saturday and—"

"And you told me you were going to visit with Trevor Heywood on Sunday. So, when do I walk down the aisle?"

She watched in surprise as Cal's cheeks reddened.

"Never with Trevor!" he growled.

"You made a rhyme," she joked, feeling a little lighter hearted. Maybe no one would be interested in her and she wouldn't have to make the decision to leave her love for Cal behind and make a new life.

"Yeah, well, that guy's a joke. Stay away from him."

"Okay."

He frowned at her. "That was easy. Aren't you going to argue or ask questions?"

"Nope. I wasn't interested in Trevor, anyway. I never liked him in school, either."

Cal's sensual lips widened in a broad smile, making her catch her breath. "Me, neither."

She returned his smile, her spirits rising because Cal was here.

He leaned toward her and she thought he was going to kiss her again. Her heartbeat doubled and her eyes widened. She wanted him to kiss her, to touch her. She wanted him to lose control, to show that at least they had one thing in common.

Even though she knew sex wouldn't solve her problem.

He sat back abruptly and cleared his throat. "Well, that leaves four men. On our list," he added, as if he thought she wasn't following the conversation.

"Yes," she agreed, licking her dry lips.

He cleared his throat again. "I have to tell you that I didn't handle Trevor well. So, I'm glad you're not disappointed."

"No, I'm not disappointed." *Relieved, actually.*

"Anyway, I know Tuck called you about the celebration Friday night."

"Yes, it's so sweet of him to want to celebrate the sale."

Cal looked embarrassed. "Baby, it's a setup for the other four men."

She stared at him, her eyes widening as she took in what he was saying. "You mean...we're not celebrating the sale?"

"Of course we are, but...but it's a good excuse to let you mingle with these guys. Not so awkward."

She clenched her jaw. She'd been pleased that her friends cared about her success. It was the only glimmer of good news she'd had since she returned from Dallas. Now, that, too, was gone. It was just a marriage trap—for a marriage she didn't want. It was Cal trying to make sure he wasn't forced into marrying her.

"I see," she finally said with no emotion. "I'm afraid I won't be able to make it."

"What? But you already told Tuck you'd be there!"

"But I don't want to come. I don't want to trick anyone into—"

"We're not tricking anyone!" Cal roared, rising. "We're giving you an opportunity to spend some time with potential husbands. That's all."

She sighed. Why was life so complicated? "Sit down, Cal. There's no need to get upset."

"If you're not coming to the party, there is," he returned, sinking back onto the sofa.

"Fine. I'll come. But I've changed my mind. I don't want you to find me a husband."

"You don't want to get married?"

"Yes! Yes, I want to get married, but...but I'll find my own husband."

"But, baby, it's dangerous out there. And now that

you've got all that money, you have to be even more careful. There are men who will wine and dine you just to get their hands on it.''

A thought suddenly struck her. ''Is that why you've never married? Because you were afraid you'd be married for your money?'' Strangely enough, that idea had never occurred to her. Probably because Cal didn't act like a rich man. But she knew he, and his parents, because of the oil discoveries twenty years ago, were wealthy.

He frowned. ''Not really. I just haven't been ready for marriage.''

''Or fatherhood?'' she said quietly.

Grinning, he said, ''My mom would kill me if I did the second without the first. You know that.''

Jessica wasn't so sure after her conversation with Mabel a week ago. Or maybe Mabel knew her son would take responsibility if he ever made a baby. Lost in the deliriously happy picture of her holding Cal's baby, she didn't realize what he said.

He touched her arm and repeated himself. ''Jess, what are you going to wear?''

''Wear?'' she questioned. Until recently he'd never discussed clothing with her. That had been the only area of her life that he ignored, until she'd worn those sexy outfits.

''Yeah. To the cookout.'' When she continued to stare at him, he said, ''You know, are you going to wear any of those man-chasing clothes?''

''No,'' she said abruptly, leaning against the back of her chair, putting as much distance as possible between them. Her daydreaming had weakened her resistance.

"No? Then what are you going to wear?"

"It's none of your business, but I'm wearing a T-shirt and jeans. That's what everyone wears to a cookout."

He nodded his head, looking pleased. "Yeah. That's good. Loose jeans."

"Loose jeans? You want me to wear baggy jeans?" She didn't own any. That's how city folks wore their jeans.

"That would be best. You know, you want to get to know these guys, let them appreciate your mind."

He was doing it again. Protecting her.

Sighing, she leaned her head back on the sofa cushion. "It doesn't matter what I wear. With you there, no one will touch me."

"Touch you? Of course not, it's a public party. You wouldn't—"

"Come on, Cal! Do you expect me to marry someone without even kissing him? This is almost the twenty-first century, not the eighteenth."

"I just want you to be careful. Some men don't listen when you say no."

"I know." She'd had a frightening experience with such a guy in college. But she'd fought him off. That wasn't a memory she was going to share with Cal, however.

But he could read her face even better than she thought.

"Did someone try that with you?" he demanded with a ferocious frown.

"It was a long time ago, Cal, and he didn't succeed," she hastily assured him.

"Someone from here? I'll haul him into jail and—"

"No. He was from Texas Tech, someone you don't know."

Before she knew what was happening, Cal had pulled her out of her chair and up into his arms. "Why didn't you tell me?" he whispered.

"What could you have done, Cal? You would've insisted I come back home."

"Damn straight! Going away to college all alone wasn't a good idea."

"You did it. Why not me?"

"Because you're a girl. And I promised your mother." His hold on her tightened.

She loved his strength, his warmth. One last time, she promised herself, and snuggled against him, her hands flat against his chest, sliding up to his neck. She let her lips touch his neck. "You've kept your promise, Cal, more than anyone could ask."

He ran his big hands over her back, pressing her even closer, while his cheek rested on her hair. Taking a deep breath, he muttered, "I keep trying, but I worry about you all the time."

She rested her face against his shoulder. "I guess that's why you want to marry me off. So I'll be someone else's responsibility."

Rearing back, he stared at her. "I'm not the one wanting you to marry. You said you wanted to, that you wanted to have kids. All this was your idea, remember?"

She remembered. Pushing out of his embrace, she paced the room, crossing her arms over her chest. She'd debated her behavior many a night.

"Jess? Have you really changed your mind?"

"I don't know!" she wailed, spinning around to stare at the most obtuse man in the world.

"Baby, what's going on? I've never known you to be so...so indecisive."

She nibbled on her bottom lip, unsure how to answer him. Finally she said, "I'm at a crossroads, Cal, and I don't know which way to go."

He gave a gentle smile, one that made her heart turn over. "Mom always says to follow your heart."

She had to turn away. "I tried that, but it involves...other people. So it's not so simple."

Cal's heart sank as he studied Jessica's rigid back. She must be talking about a particular man. He hadn't realized Jessica had a guy in mind for her future plans. Why had they developed a list? Unless the man was already on it....

"Is it someone you know?"

She turned to look at him, her eyes wide. "What?"

"Is the man you want to marry someone you know?"

"Of course he is!" she snapped. "I'd be pretty stupid to pine for a stranger." Then her eyes widened even more and her hand covered her mouth, as if she regretted what she'd just admitted.

"Is he on the list?"

"I don't want to talk about this."

He strode to her side, but he managed to keep his hands to himself. "How can I help you if you don't tell me who you want?"

She turned away from him. "You can't help me, Cal."

"Yeah, I could." He cupped her shoulders and settled her warm body against him, burying his nose in her hair. "I could tell him you're…a wonderful lady. I could point out what a good wife you'd make."

Pulling away from him, she crossed the room before she faced him. "And you think those facts would make a man love me?"

"Of course they would!"

She smiled sadly, wrapping her arms around her taut body. "It's not that easy, Cal. A man…a man has to want to marry, to settle down, before he even thinks about a woman that way." Her gaze flew away from him. "My man doesn't."

My man. Those words tore at Cal's heart. Those same words had described him a few days ago. Until he'd awakened to his feelings for Jessica. Him and his friends.

Like a lightning bolt, his last thought flashed through his mind. His friends… That's why Jess wouldn't talk to him, wouldn't reveal the name of the man she loved. The man she wanted to marry had to be one of his three friends. And of his three friends, the one most resistant to marriage was Mac.

Cal loved Tuck, Spence, and Mac like brothers; he'd shared everything with them through the years. But he and Mac were particularly close, ever since they'd been on their own in Dallas. He'd lived through Mac's marriage and the disastrous divorce that followed.

He'd never forget the night Mac had called him and asked him to meet him at a crowded, dark bar, a place they almost never frequented. Mac had wanted to talk about his marriage ending, and he hadn't wanted anyone to overhear. That painful evening was etched on Cal's heart.

Mac had vowed then he'd never tread those waters again. And Cal was pretty sure he wouldn't. But if anyone could persuade him, it would be Jess.

He almost rubbed his chest to ease the pain he felt there. Not only would he lose Jessica to another man, but he'd have to watch their happiness from close quarters.

Could he bear it?

He squared his jaw and said quietly, "Tell me who he is, baby," seeking confirmation from Jessica, "and I'll help you. We'll hog-tie him in no time. And you'll be happy."

Chapter Eight

Prior to Friday night's party, Cal returned to Mac's home. Now that he had figured out it was Mac that Jessica wanted, he had to do something. Even if she'd refused to confide in him.

He didn't blame her. Mac was a great guy. Financially, all four of them were set, but Mac, because of his law degree, had earning potential even if there was a financial disaster.

He was also the most determined against marriage. That must be why Jess was so sure her case was hopeless.

Not with Cal helping her.

His friend would have to give up his resistance to marriage. Jessica had to be happy. And Cal was resigned to a lot of suffering on his part.

"Everything ready for tonight?" Mac asked as Cal sat down.

"Mostly. But something occurred to me, and I figured you could help me out."

"Sure, Cal, whatever you need."

"I want you to stick close to Jess tonight."

Mac frowned. "I thought that was your job. You're the one who—"

"That's why it has to be you."

"What are you talking about?"

"If I stick close to Jess, all the men will keep away. I've threatened most of them at one time or another. They won't have forgotten." He grimaced. Jess was right. He'd done too good a job.

"Hmm," Mac said. "You could be right. Okay, I'll keep an eye on her."

"Unless you've got plans with another woman." Cal watched Mac closely.

His eyebrows shot up. "Another woman? You think I've changed my mind about marrying?"

"You seemed real enthusiastic about Jess's change of heart." Cal leaned against the back of the chair, trying to look casual. "Maybe marriage isn't such a bad idea."

"Are we searching for your wife next? I think you should marry Jess and keep everything simple."

Cal's face flooded with color. "I wish you guys would stop suggesting such a thing. That's not what Jess wants."

"What do *you* want?"

His answer was simple. In spite of the complicated emotions he was beginning to feel for Jessica, he knew what he wanted. "I want her to be happy."

Mac sent him a surrender grin. "Okay, I'll do my duty. But, Cal, I'm not going to be as rigorous as you. I expect a man to touch her, you know."

Cal frowned. Mac must not be as interested as he'd hoped, because he knew he'd flatten anyone who dared lay a finger on Jess. "You're probably right," he said slowly, keeping a smile on his face, though the words hurt. "Maybe you should, you know, hug her…or kiss her a time or two to give the others an idea."

Mac laughed. "I don't think any of the men in Cactus need that kind of instruction."

"No, but it might give them the idea that…that I'm not guarding Jessica anymore."

"But it might give Jessica the wrong idea. She's a sweetheart, but I wouldn't mislead her for anything. And you, of all people, know I never intend to marry again."

Cal nodded. He remembered. And this conversation was killing him. But he kept Jessica's happiness in his sights. "Just a kiss or two. For me."

JESSICA HAD SPENT the day at Florence Gibbons's house, leaving just a few minutes before Cal had arrived, unaware of his enlistment of Mac's services.

After a shower, she pulled on her jeans and T-shirt, in a much better mood for the first time since the sale of her restaurants. She'd devised a new steak sauce and she and Florence had marinated the meat for this evening.

A new idea was swirling around in her brain. When Alex had arrived, a few minutes earlier, she ran it by the attorney to be sure she wouldn't be abusing the noncompetition clause.

"No, you're okay," Alex had informed her. "We made the noncompetition clause applicable to Mexican restaurants only. Give it an American name, don't serve nachos, and you're home free. Are you really going to do it?"

"Wait until you taste the steaks tonight, and you tell me." But Jessica knew. She was excited about her new recipe. And she was excited to have something else to think about besides Cal.

When she emerged from her bedroom, her long hair tied back with a green scarf to match her green T-shirt, Alex was waiting for her.

"I hope you didn't mind the long drive. Tuck thought it was important that you be here for the celebration." She watched in surprise as Alex's cheeks reddened.

"Not at all. It was a good excuse to skip work today. The long drive gave me some time to think. Burnout is becoming a distinct possibility."

"Really? You're always so enthusiastic, I assumed you love your work."

"I do! At least, I would. Most of the time I'm so busy I don't have time to enjoy anything. And most of my clients aren't as much fun as you." Alex ran her hand through her thick, blond pageboy and sighed. "I'm kind of confused right now."

"Join the crowd. I feel like I've been cut adrift in the middle of the ocean."

"Do you regret the sale?"

"No. I'd gone as far as I could go with The Old Cantina. If my new idea works, it'll be a new challenge, something to occupy myself with."

"And since you made so much money, you don't have to be quite so anxious about it succeeding," Alex pointed out.

"No money worries. Just personal pride."

"Yeah," her attorney agreed, almost as if she faced the same thing.

"Shall we go? I want to get there early and make sure the steaks are properly cooked." It was only five o'clock. It wouldn't be dark for another hour, but Alex seemed as eager to go as she was.

When they arrived at the Langford ranch, it appeared others had wanted to arrive early, too. At least a dozen vehicles, mostly trucks, were parked in front of the house.

"Looks like we're going to have a good turnout," Jessica murmured.

"Is that unusual?"

"Not really. Out here, when someone has a big party like this, everyone assumes they're invited whether they are or not." She grinned at the city girl beside her. "I hope you wore your dancing shoes. There's sure to be a fiddler or two in the bunch, and the Langfords have a great deck for dancing."

"Will they build the bonfire that close to the house?" Alex asked, frowning.

"It won't be that close. And there'll be plenty of men keeping an eye on it. Grass fires are a serious thing out here. We don't get a lot of rainfall. But after we eat, they'll move the party to the deck."

They entered the front of the house without knocking. Most of the guests were going around, heading for the pile of wood that was already starting to flame up. But Jessica wanted to check the meat.

"Howdy, Jess," Ruth Langford said with a smile. "Who's this pretty lady?"

Jessica introduced Alex to Tuck's mother, Mabel, Florence, and Edith Hauk. "I wanted to check on the steaks. How do they look?" Jessica asked Florence.

"Good. I can't wait."

Jess opened the refrigerator door and stared at the meat on trays. Then she lifted the plastic wrap and sniffed. "Perfect."

"Is this a special recipe?" Mabel asked.

"A brand-new one. Let me know what you think."

The excitement in her voice must've given her away.

"You got something on your mind?" Mabel asked. "Something to do with steaks?"

"Maybe," Jessica returned with a smile. "I'm not saying anything else. Just let me know what you think."

"We won't have to tell you, honey," Florence said. "Just see how quick those boys wolf them down. That'll be the answer."

"I don't know. Seems to me you could cook leather and they'd wolf it down. They're human eating machines," Jessica teased, since all four women could claim one of those eating machines.

"Hey, where are the steaks?" Tuck roared from the back door.

"Speak of the devil," Ruth said with a laugh, opening the refrigerator again and pulling out one of the long trays. "Jess, you want to take this one? And, Alex? Can we draft you? We have six trays and there are six of us."

Jessica led the way. She wanted to check the placement of the grill before any of the meat went on the fire.

"Jess!" Tuck exclaimed as she appeared, but she noticed his gaze slipped past her to Alex. "I didn't know you were here."

"We're here. I want to see the grill before we start

cooking." She went past him, not surprised that he waited for Alex and took the tray away from her. He was always a gentleman.

"Hey, Jess, you're not cooking tonight," Tuck called from behind her. "I am. We wouldn't ask you to cook your own celebration dinner."

She ignored his protest. "It wouldn't be the first time. Besides, it's what I want to do."

As they approached the fire, she was surprised to see that Cal remain seated on a nearby log while Mac stood and came toward her. What was up?

As she got closer she realized Cal was visiting with Melanie Rule, a friend who worked in the drugstore. Was Cal interested in Melanie?

"Hey, Jess, need some help?" Mac asked, reaching out his strong arms for the long tray.

"Thanks, Mac. I want to check the grill before I put the steaks on."

Mac protested, with Tuck's repeated words, that she wasn't doing the cooking. Jessica just smiled.

The grill was six feet by three feet of heavy metal that Tuck's father had had made specially for outdoor grilling. It was laid on top of two logs and coals were raked out of the fire beneath it.

"Looks like your pile of wood has been burning for a while. Those are great coals," Jessica observed, trying to keep her gaze from flying to Cal. He hadn't moved from his place beside Melanie.

Mac was the only one to answer. "Uh, yeah, Tuck started it about an hour ago."

Jessica looked over her shoulder to find Tuck and Alex in an involved discussion. She decided Alex could handle Tuck, so she turned her attention back to the meat. "The steaks are ready." With a long fork, she began laying them on the grill.

"HOW WAS YOUR DRIVE?" Tuck asked, his voice soft as he leaned toward Alex.

"Fine."

"It's good to see you again." Hell, he was practically panting. And no wonder. She was wearing a T-shirt and jeans that were formfitting.

"You, too," she said with a smile, but he wanted more. He wanted to see hunger in her eyes like the hunger that was in his gut.

He wanted her. Not to marry, of course. In spite of his teasing Cal and the others, he had no intention of marrying. At least not for a while.

Life was good. He didn't want it to change. But the last few weeks, he'd been unable to forget Alex.

"Want to visit the barn? Joey missed you." He'd introduced Alex to his favorite horse when she'd toured his ranch earlier.

He'd also introduced Alex to making out in a hay barn. A very satisfying experience. Male pride filled him as her cheeks darkened. She remembered.

"Do we have time before dinner? I'd like to see Joey again."

"I think we have a little time," he said, keeping his tone casual even as his pulse speeded up. He grabbed her hand and headed toward the barn, not caring who was watching. He was about to put his stamp on the lovely Alex…again.

JESSICA HAD THREE ROWS of big steaks already sizzling when Cal approached her. Nonchalantly, she looked up, expecting Melanie to be at his side. Instead, he was alone.

"How's it going?" he asked, but she noted his gaze left her and traveled almost immediately to Mac.

"Great," Mac replied. "These steaks smell wonderful. Aunt Flo must've put some kind of special seasoning on them."

Cal put his hands on his hips and muttered, "I didn't mean the food."

Jessica looked at him sharply. What had he meant, then? She ducked her head again and remained silent, hoping Cal might forget she was there.

"She just got here," Mac said softly.

"Yeah, but—"

"Howdy, Jessie," Trevor Heywood boomed from behind Jessica.

She hated being called Jessie. With a cool look over her shoulder, she replied, "Hey, Woodie."

"Don't call me that!" he snapped.

"Don't call me Jessie," she returned without emotion.

"Sorry. I forgot. Say, let's get together and talk later this evening. I've got some good ideas for investments and I hear you've got a few dollars to put away." A genial smile didn't hide the greed in his eyes.

"Thanks for the offer, but I have a bank in Dallas handling my investments."

"Those banks don't give personal attention to a small amount like you have, so—"

Alex, who'd disappeared with Tuck for a few minutes and then returned, her hair slightly mussed, laughed. "You obviously don't know the value of Jessica's restaurants, Mr. Heywood, if you think that. I can assure you any bank in Dallas would give Jessica all the attention she can stand."

Jessica almost laughed out loud at the chagrin on Trevor's face. But he made a quick recovery. "That's great. Maybe you should diversify. You know, invest some in Dallas, and some here in Cactus. Support your hometown, you know."

"Thanks for the offer, but we're here to celebrate, not talk business," she said gently. Then she turned her back on him and filled in the space left on the grill with meat. "That's it," she said. "We should be ready to eat in a few minutes."

"Time to turn the lights on," Tuck said as he joined them again. He headed back to the house. They'd strung lights in a square near the bonfire and picnic tables and benches were waiting for the guests.

Alex stared around her. "Good heavens. This is a major undertaking."

"We don't do things small out here," Jessica said with a grin. All the time, her mind was coming up with tidbits for the future.

She excused herself and began moving among the people gathered, giving them a chance to greet and congratulate her.

When she noticed Mac following her around, she frowned at him. "What is it, Mac? Did you want to ask me something?"

He took a step back. "No. I thought I'd say hello to everyone."

"Oh." She was about to move away when Kevin Lancaster approached her.

"Hello, Jess. It's good news about your sale. I guess you won't have to worry about work for a little while."

Though she realized the man was fishing for information about her financial windfall, she answered him blandly. "For a month or two."

"Good, good. That's better than ranching. With beef prices, you never know if you're going to make a profit or not."

"Agriculture is always that way, isn't it? Though I'll have to tell you the restaurant business isn't very stable, either," she added.

Mac, still beside her, said, "Jess happens to have a lot of talent."

She flashed him a smile of thanks. Which distracted her from Cal's approach.

"You'd probably do better if you had a wife to help you, Kevin. Someone who could cook for the hands and make roundup more enticing to the rest of us." Cal slung his arm around Jessica's shoulders. "Like Jess, here."

Jessica's cheeks flushed and she turned to glare at Cal, only to find him staring at Mac, not Kevin.

"Uh, yeah," Mac responded tardily. "Jess is certainly a good cook."

She felt like a side of beef hanging in a meat market. Not a pleasant feeling. "I think I'd better check on the steaks."

"Tuck's taking care of them," Cal protested.

She didn't bother to contradict him. With a murmured "Excuse me," she marched away from the three men. And discovered that Tuck was nowhere in sight and the steaks were ready to be turned over.

She busied herself with the meat, happy to be alone. When she was finished, she looked around for Alex, but she didn't see her. "Mabel, have you seen Alex?"

"No, Jess, I haven't. How much longer for the steaks?"

"About five minutes. Can I help with anything else?"

"No, no, it's your party. Go mingle."

Jessica saw Melanie Rule sitting alone at one of the tables. Melanie had no family in the area and she worked hard. Jessica liked her.

And if Cal was interested in her, then Jessica was determined to be friends with her, even if it killed her.

"Melanie, how are you?" she asked, sitting next to her.

"Fine, Jess. Congratulations."

"Thanks."

"I guess you don't have to worry about money anymore," Melanie said with a sigh.

Jessica knew Melanie had no family support that she knew of and her job at the drugstore probably didn't pay very high wages, but truthfully she was getting tired of everyone's comments about her financial status. "No, not really," she admitted with a sympathetic smile.

"Some people have all the luck," Melanie said with a determined smile. "First your restaurants and then Cal."

"Cal? What are you talking about? Cal is a friend."

Melanie studied her, as if considering her next words, but before she could speak, they were interrupted by Jerry Brockmeier, the owner of the drugstore.

"Hey, there, ladies," he greeted, sliding onto the bench across from them. "Congratulations, Jessica. I've got some new stuff in from Dallas you might want to come spend your fortune on," he said with a big grin. "Some of that good fake diamond stuff. Cubic zirconia."

Melanie seemed embarrassed at Jerry's crass self-promotion, but Jessica had known him all her life. He'd been a couple of years older than her, between Cal and her grades. He'd inherited the drugstore from his father when he'd died. He and his mother ran it, with only a few employees, like Melanie.

"Thanks, Jerry, but I'm not much for jewelry."

"She'd probably like a ring for her third finger," Cal said from behind Jessica. When she whirled around and glared at him, he added, "Most ladies do."

Jerry, fortunately, didn't take the hint the way Cal intended. "Hey, send the lucky guy in, and I'll sell him a great ring."

"There is no one, Jerry. Cal is just teasing."

"But there might be soon," Cal added. "Where's Mac?"

Jessica frowned at him. "I don't know. I left him with you."

"Well, darn it..." Cal began.

"Hey, Jess, how are you?" Spence asked, interrupting his friend. "Hi, Melanie. Jerry."

There were general greetings, then Spence said, "Melanie, want to come take a look at some puppies Tuck has? They're in the barn."

Melanie didn't exhibit a lot of enthusiasm, but she stood. "Yes, of course. Cal, do you want to see the puppies?"

Jessica cringed at the hopeful expression in her friend's gaze. Yes, Cal had made an impression on Melanie. Not that Jessica was surprised. Most women fell for him at once.

She thought it was that combination of muscle and heart, strength and caring. And life hadn't been easy for Melanie.

Cal frowned. "If I knew where Mac was, I'd like—"

"You need Mac to look at puppies?" Jessica questioned. This was the second time she'd gotten the feeling that Cal had arranged something with Mac.

"No, I..." Cal began, looking embarrassed.

"Come on, Cal. Melanie wants you to come," Spence stated firmly.

With a shrug, and a glare at Jerry, Cal walked off with the other two.

"Is he mad at me? I don't want any trouble with the sheriff," Jerry protested.

"No, of course not. He believes in preventive frowns," Jessica assured him.

"So, are you planning to get married, like Cal said?" Jerry asked. "You've never dated a home-grown boy, have you?"

"No, and we all know why." Jessica didn't bother pretending it had been her choice.

Jerry relaxed and smiled. "I guess so. Cal's pretty persuasive."

"Yeah. I've got to go check the steaks. Good to see you, Jerry."

"Yeah. Say, come by for a soda some afternoon."

He and his mother still had an old-fashioned ice cream and hamburger bar in the drugstore.

"Thanks, Jerry, I'll do that."

She returned to the fire. Still no sign of Tuck. Some chef he was! She certainly wouldn't hire him for her new venture. That brought a chuckle to her lips. As if he'd be interested.

Several ladies stepped forward to help as she began putting steaks on plates. The four hostesses, drafted by their sons, brought out the vegetables and bread, and the tables filled up quickly.

As Jessica finished serving the steaks, she listened to the comments filtering through the night air. In addition to the contented silence, there were some rave reviews she enjoyed.

Yes, she thought, her idea was going to work.

"What are you up to?" Cal demanded.

Chapter Nine

Cal's eyes narrowed when Jess jumped at his question.

"Um, taking the steaks off the fire."

"You're not supposed to be cooking. Where's Mac?"

She raised her eyebrows. "I don't know. Tuck was supposed to be in charge of the steaks, but I haven't seen him anywhere."

Tuck? Was she interested in Tuck? No, that wasn't love in her voice. It was irritation.

Before he could decide who to look for, Mac hurried up.

"Sorry, Cal, but old man Jones has a legal problem and he wanted to discuss it with me."

"Tell him you're busy and he should make an appointment." Cal glared at his friend. Mac wasn't fulfilling his role very well. And he wasn't showing any signs of falling for Jess.

Deciding to give Mac another chance, Cal said, "Here, Jess, I'll finish serving the steaks. You and Mac take yours and go grab a table." Cal stepped to her side and slid his hand over the handle of the long fork she was using. When his skin touched hers, he fought back an urge to pull her into his arms.

"No, I want to finish," she protested, refusing to give the fork to him.

"It's your party. You're not supposed to cook," he repeated. He looked around for support from Mac and discovered he was gone. "Where'd Mac go?"

"I think he's helping his aunt set up another table," Jessica said, elbowing Cal out of her way. Then she handed him a plate filled with steaming beef. "Here, go eat."

"I'll wait for you." If Mac wasn't going to keep an eye on her, as he'd promised, Cal would have to take over.

"Fine. Everyone's been served, so I'm ready."

Cal checked the area and located two seats at the table where Tony Brewster, the local minister, and the last man on the list, was seated. It might be good to test Jessica's reaction to the man.

Just in case he'd been wrong about Mac.

JESSICA CUT A PIECE of meat and put it in her mouth, fear warring with pride. What if it tasted terrible?

Even as she chewed, relief filling her, she watched Cal and the others at the table. Cal ate his first bite, then turned to her.

"Jess, this steak is great. What did you put on it?"

"That's a trade secret," she assured him, smiling.

Reverend Brewster smiled at her. "Whatever the secret is, guard it well, Jessica. It could make you another fortune."

"Thanks, I will," she said with a big smile.

"Jess isn't interested in another restaurant, Tony," Cal hurriedly said. "She has other plans."

Jessica stared at him, unable to believe his words.

Tony leaned forward. "Oh, really? What plans, Jessica?"

Jessica tried to think of an appropriate response. She moved her lips several times, but nothing came out.

Cal had no such problem. "Jess is thinking about settling down. You know, starting a family." He stared at Tony. "Don't you think that's a good idea, Tony?"

Jessica closed her eyes. Cal might as well paint a bull's-eye on her back. Subtlety wasn't his strong point. But then, it never had been. He'd always been starkly honest.

"A great idea. Who's the lucky man, Jessica?"

Did she dare? It was the third time tonight that Cal had pushed her into a difficult situation. Maybe it was time he learned to mind his own business.

"Well," she said with a smile at Tony, "I'm either going to start a new restaurant or marry Cal. I haven't decided."

CAL CHOKED on his steak. Somehow, he suspected Jessica's hearty whacks to his back held punishment rather than sympathy. But for what? He'd just been trying to help.

Once he could breathe again, he interrupted Tony's congratulations. "She's teasing you, Tony."

"You mean, you're turning me down?" Jessica asked, pouring all her sixth-grade dramatic training into her voice and expression.

"Watch it, baby, or you're going to be in trouble," he warned, leaning toward her.

"Oh, well, then I guess I'll have to start a new restaurant," she assured her audience, shrugging her shoulders and grinning, as if that had been her intent all along.

Everyone began asking questions about her plans, accepting her remark about marrying Cal as a joke.

Cal stared at her. She'd told him she wanted to marry, start a family. She wouldn't have time if she opened another restaurant. What was going on? Had she completely changed her mind? He'd thought it was because she didn't like the names on his list.

They were going to have to have a long talk.

The first opportunity came when the party moved to the deck and Tim Collishaw picked up his fiddle. Jessica was standing among some of the women, discussing her recipe and her plans.

Cal walked to her side, slid his hand around her waist. "Come on, Jess. As the honoree, you need to start the dancing." The temptation to slide his hand beneath her green T-shirt, to feel the warmth of her skin with his, was hard to resist.

"No, I—"

"No choice, baby," he whispered in her ear as he pulled her to the center of the deck. With everyone watching, he knew she wouldn't refuse him now.

But he didn't want only the two of them dancing, everyone's gaze on them. As he wrapped his arms around her, he called to the crowd, "Join us, folks."

Men and women filled the deck until there was scarcely room to move. That satisfied Cal. He didn't have much interest in dance moves.

"What's going on, baby?" he whispered, bending to Jess's ear.

With a grin that told him she wasn't interested in any serious talk, she said, "We're dancing. And not too well if you can't even figure out what's going on."

"You know what I mean. What's this idea about another restaurant? I thought you wanted a family."

Her smile faded and she leaned her forehead against his shoulder.

"Jess?"

"I don't want to talk now," she muttered.

Cal pulled her closer to him, their bodies touching from knee to shoulder. He loved the feel of her against him, her scent enveloping him. Talk? No, that wasn't what was on his mind, either.

He guessed Jess didn't know how much her closeness affected his body. Since she kissed him that first time, he was discovering a craving for her touch, her kisses. They'd been friends forever, but now he wanted more.

But he couldn't take what she didn't want to offer.

So he held her.

And swayed to the music that he hoped would never end.

"DO YOU THINK he'll marry her?" Florence asked Mabel softly as they watched the dancing.

Mabel kept her gaze pinned on her two children, Cal and Jessica. "I don't know."

"I want to win," Florence said with determination, "but I hope those two get together. They were made for each other."

"I know. The bet doesn't matter, you know that. But it's made us finally do something. I think that bet was the smartest thing we've ever done."

"You could be right, for everyone but Mac. That boy has the hardest head I've ever seen."

"Where is he?"

"Sitting over there talking about a law case with Herk Jones. Can you believe that? All these beautiful young women, and he talks to an old man."

"But I thought you had a plan?"

"I did. I was going to invite my godchild to visit. I thought Mac would be attracted to her."

"What happened?"

"She got engaged," Florence said with disgust. "She called to tell me her exciting news the night I intended to call. Thank goodness, she told me before I invited her to come. That would've been a totally wasted visit, with her already in love with someone else."

"So now what?" Mabel asked, still watching the pair on the dance floor.

"I have no idea. I'm gonna say my prayers and hope God takes pity on me."

CAL WAS GLAD the lights were low. When the music ended, he figured his need for Jessica would be obvious to everyone unless he remained in the shadows. He was ashamed at the way his body reacted to her, when he was supposed to be her protector, but he didn't know how to stop it.

He directed them toward the steps that led down to the lawn and darkness. Just as the music ended, he lifted her against him and stepped down.

Her head came up. "What are you doing?"

"Giving someone else the chance to dance."

"Oh."

"You okay?"

"Of course."

"Are you really going to open a restaurant?"

"I have to do something, Cal. I've been going crazy sitting at home."

"But you haven't given this marriage idea a chance. I've never known you to give up so easily. You wouldn't even tell me who you want so I could help."

"Because I told you I didn't want any help. And tonight, you might as well have painted a sign to hang on my back—Woman Wants Husband!"

"But you said you did."

"That didn't mean I wanted everyone in Cactus to know that."

"I think they're all interested," he went on, ignoring her protest. "But I'm afraid some of them are more interested in your money than you. No offense, baby. They're pretty dumb to feel that way."

Her slender hand cupped his cheek. "Thanks, Cal. But you're right. The whole town wants to know how much I got to the penny." She sighed. "I guess I understand the four of you not marrying."

"The four of who?"

"You, Mac, Spence, and Tuck. You have to worry about whether it's you or your oil wells."

Cal studied her, then tried out his theory. "I guess any of those guys would make a good husband for you, since you wouldn't have to worry about them marrying you for your money."

"And you." Her cheeks flushed. "The three of them and you."

"Yeah," he agreed. "And me. Too bad we're more like brother and sister." He flexed his suddenly aching shoulders, as if he were holding himself too rigid. "But Mac and the others don't consider you to be their sister. You're just a good friend."

"That's nice," she said with a sigh. Then, as if he hadn't brought up the subject of her marrying, she added, "But I'm very excited about my new restaurant idea."

He wasn't going to let her squirm away this time. "Look, baby, I've been thinking—"

She whirled around to face him, an expectant look on her face. "Yes?"

"Well, I mean, Mac or…or Spence or Tuck would make a good husband."

The light went out of her face and she turned away. "I need to talk to Mabel." Then, as she passed Melanie Rule, she stopped. "Cal?"

"Yes, baby?"

"Why don't you dance with Melanie? She's a very good dancer." Then she walked off.

Since Cal was a gentleman, and Melanie had overheard Jessica's words, he had no choice. But his attention remained on Jessica rather than the lady in his arms.

SPENCE STOOD in the shadows and watched the dancers on Tuck's deck. In particular, his gaze focused on Cal and his partner. What a mess.

Melanie Rule was an attractive lady. Spence had noticed her lately. She'd only moved to Cactus a couple of years ago, and she was quiet. Almost withdrawn.

He'd thought about asking her out. Until he'd seen the way she looked at Cal.

So Melanie was keeping an eye on Cal, and he was keeping an eye on Jess, and Spence didn't know who Jess was keeping an eye on.

Spence had accepted Mac's warnings about marriage. At least for now. Someday, he intended to have a family. But it wouldn't be someone who loved one of his friends. He knew that problem would be the kiss of death to a marriage.

He felt sympathy for Melanie.

But not enough to get involved in a threesome.

JESSICA SPENT THE WEEKEND wandering around her town house with a yellow pad, making notes for her new project. It was easier to concentrate on her business life than her personal life, which was a disaster.

Her plan to awaken Cal to her love for him hadn't worked. He seemed more intent than ever on finding her a husband, even offering to sacrifice his best friends. Which meant he didn't want her, because she'd been more than obvious.

On Monday, she began checking out locations. She'd decided to call her restaurant The Last Roundup. When she found a wooden building on the town square big enough to accommodate the kitchen, a large dining area and a second room where she intended to have a live band and dance floor, she contacted the owner.

Since economic growth in Cactus had leveled off the last few years, the owner was thrilled at the opportunity to sell his property. Jessica called the architect in Lubbock she'd used for her other restaurants, and he made a trip out to Cactus to check out the property.

Then she took him to The Old Cantina for lunch.

Jeffrey Lockheart was a talented architect. Jessica had discovered him about five years ago when she'd had a problem with one of the buildings she'd bought.

"Do you think it will take much rebuilding to bring the place up to standard?" she asked as they dined.

"Not too much. We'll need to get the foundation repaired. Of course, a lot of the wood will have to be replaced. I assume you want—"

"Mornin', Jess," Cal drawled from over her shoulder. "Is this a private luncheon?"

She smiled. "Not that private. Have you met Jeff?" Introducing the two men, explaining Jeff's presence, Jessica smiled at Cal's obvious relief. What had he thought?

"You're the sheriff?" Jeff asked.

Cal nodded. "Yeah. I try to keep tabs on everything. I don't know why I haven't met you before now."

"I didn't start working with Jessica until her fourth restaurant. All of those were out of town. This will be my first job in Cactus."

Leaning forward, toward Jessica, Cal directed his question to her. "So you're going to go ahead? Is it legal? Didn't you sign a contract not to compete?"

"I can't open a Mexican-themed restaurant. Instead, I'm opening a steak house." She hoped he didn't bring her personal life into the discussion.

"Your new recipe?"

"Yes."

Jeff was staring at first Cal and then Jessica, as if puzzled.

"What is it, Jeff?" she asked.

"I'm just amazed. I didn't realize a sheriff would worry about you breaking your contract. Crime must be really low in small towns."

Jessica couldn't hold back a grin and Cal chuckled. She nodded toward Cal to respond to Jeff's misconception.

"There's as much crime here as anywhere. Jess and I are friends. I wasn't asking in an official capacity." He scooted his chair a little closer to Jessica, as if to physically link the two of them.

Jeff smiled in return. "Still, I think I'll bring my wife to visit Cactus. I'd like her to see how pleasant it can be."

"You're married?" Cal returned, looking a little happier to have Jeff in his town.

"Yeah, married with two kids."

Cal extended his arm across the back of Jessica's chair. "Great. That's a great idea to bring them here."

Nita, the waitress who usually served Jessica and her friends, delivered a plate of nachos and drinks for Jeff and Jessica. Noting Cal's arrival, she promised to bring him a soda, since he was on duty.

"How are you doing, Nita?" Jessica asked. One condition of her sale had been the new owners' retention of her staff.

"Okay. It's a little different than when you were my boss, but we're okay."

"Great."

"What are you doing with yourself? Don't you miss it?"

"Yeah, but I'm thinking of opening a different kind of restaurant." Jessica regretted her words as soon as she said them, but she wasn't good at keeping secrets.

"Hey, maybe I could move to your new place," Nita suggested.

"We'll see," Jessica said, but she worried that the corporation that had bought her restaurant chain might feel she wasn't holding to the spirit of their agreement.

Cal's fingers rubbed her shoulder, as if to soothe her nerves. Somehow his touch did reassure her, but at the same time it electrified her nerve endings, making heat rise in her.

Cal brought back the topic of her restaurant after Nita left the table. "So where's this new restaurant going to be located? And what are you calling it?"

Jeff deferred to her, since it was her project, but Jessica was reluctant to reveal her plans. "I'm not ready to talk about it yet."

Cal removed his arm from the back of her chair and stared at her. "With me?"

She looked away. "Nothing's settled yet."

"You think you can't trust me?"

Hearing the hurt in his voice, she turned to look at him. "You know that's not what I mean." She leaned forward, drawing imaginary circles on the table.

"Then why not tell me?" Cal demanded. "Haven't you already told Jeff?"

She had, and couldn't explain why she wasn't ready to tell Cal. Now she had no choice if she wasn't going to hurt his feelings. "Okay, fine. I'm thinking of the name The Last Roundup. I'm going to have food and music, with a live band, a dance floor."

"Kind of like Friday night," Cal said, nodding. "Can't get better than that."

He was right about that. Dancing with Cal had made the evening perfect. Somehow she didn't think dancing with Cal would be a part of her future. He'd spent some time after their dance with Melanie Rule. That was the second time he'd singled the lady out for special attention.

After they finished their meal, Jeff excused himself, needing to get back to Lubbock. Cal didn't show any sign of leaving.

"I thought he was the guy you wanted," Cal muttered, reaching for another chip. The relief that had filled him when Jeff had mentioned his wife and two children had almost overwhelmed him.

"What?"

"One of my guys told me you were wandering around town with a stranger, a good-looking man. I thought he was the man you were pining after." He'd hit the door in seconds, panic filling him. Panic that told him something about himself he hadn't wanted to admit.

Jessica rolled her eyes. "Really, Cal, just because I speak to a man doesn't mean—"

Before she could complete her protest, Trevor

Heywood stopped by their table. "Hey, Jessica, didn't think I'd see you here."

"Why not? The Old Cantina is still the best restaurant in town," she replied, smiling coolly.

"True. Say, how about dinner one night this week? We could discuss your investments, your future. And maybe each other," he added, his face flushing.

"Thanks, Trevor, but I've got another project going and it's going to take up all my time." She continued to smile, as if Trevor's disappointment didn't bother her.

Cal was pleased.

"Gee, thanks, Cal. Trevor pursuing me is all I need."

"Hey, you approved the list. And I was only trying to help." But not anymore. He turned around as someone called out his name.

Cal almost groaned. The only man on the list he hadn't tried to interest had just come into the restaurant. Richard West had established himself as a leading builder of basic functional houses in the area.

"Richard, how are you?" Cal asked as he stood and shook hands. "You remember Jessica Hoya, don't you?"

"Of course I do. Who could forget a beautiful woman like Jessica?"

Jessica smiled and shook hands, but she didn't appear flustered by Richard's lavish compliment.

"Why don't you join us?" Cal asked.

Jessica abruptly stood. "I'm afraid I have to talk to Nita, if you'll excuse me. But it was nice to see you again, Richard."

"Then join *me*," Cal said to Richard, having no choice. The man was an old friend. He couldn't be rude to him.

He regretted his friendliness at once.

Richard leaned forward and said softly, "I hear Jessica is free and looking."

Cal froze. He hadn't expected a direct question. "Uh, I don't know."

"Come on, Cal, who would know if you didn't? You two have always been tight."

Scowling at his friend, Cal finally said, "You'll have to ask Jessica." And he hoped she sent Richard packing as fast as she had the others.

When Jessica returned to the table a few minutes later, Richard had already excused himself and disappeared. Cal watched her cross the restaurant, his mind teeming with questions.

"Obviously the man you're interested in isn't Richard," he said as she sat down. "So, tell me who it is."

"It's a new restaurant, remember?"

"A new restaurant can't give you a baby. It won't keep you warm at night, or love you for the rest of your life." As he wanted to do. He wanted to hold Jessica in his arms for the rest of his life. He wanted to be one with her, to give her those babies.

Jessica looked away, her lashes beating almost as fast as a hummingbird's wings. "My, my, you sound almost like a poet, Cal. Maybe you're the one who should consider marriage instead of me."

"Maybe I should."

Chapter Ten

Cal spent a lot of time thinking. Everything around him seemed to have changed. Particularly Jessica. Now that he'd been forced to realize that Jessica wasn't a child anymore, he knew she was right. She should marry and have children.

The most startling realization, however, was that he wanted to be the father of her children.

Though it was a ridiculous comparison, he felt like Sleeping Beauty, awakened with a kiss from Jessica. Had his protection, all these years, been jealousy? Had his shooing away suitors been a selfish act?

He didn't know.

All he knew now was how much he wanted Jessica in his life. How much he wanted her in his family. How much he wanted her in his bed.

After all these years of refusing to think of marriage, it was all that occupied his mind these days. Marriage and Jessica. A sharing of their lives.

How appropriate when they'd spent their first years together, sharing the joys and pains. Jessica's first birthday after their meeting, when she turned five, was a special memory. Mabel had baked a cake and Cal had worked hard to make Jessica a small leather coin purse.

He'd learned to carve leather in Boy Scouts and he'd done her initials intertwined with flowers. When her green eyes had glowed with pride, his heart had almost burst. His father had given her some coins to put in the little purse, and she'd carried it with her everywhere.

When he'd broken his arm three years later, she'd spent a lot of the summer comforting him, reading to him, letting him teach her about ranching. He'd gotten so distracted by her earnest questions, he'd forgotten the pain and boredom that bothered him.

He was looking at his future with the same pain and boredom without Jessica. Life without Jessica in Cactus, or anywhere else for that matter, had no meaning.

Cal had always been an action kind of guy. Now he was forced to think about what he intended to do. How was he going to convince Jessica that he was the perfect one for her plan? The perfect father for her babies. The perfect man to make those babies.

And that thought, one he arrived at regularly, halted all rational thinking. Because his mind would drift off into pictures of the two of them entwined, their bodies slick with perspiration and sated with pleasure.

He could almost feel her silken hair, his fingers wrapped in it. Her scent filled his nostrils even in the barn because he was thinking of her instead of the animals. He saw her glowing eyes rather than the stars at night.

He was still debating how he could convince Jessica, especially since she seemed to be avoiding him, when she stormed into the barn the next Saturday morning.

His friends, Mac, Tuck, and Spence, had come to help him unload hay he'd purchased for the winter. Tuck and Spence were on the truck, tossing down the bales, while he and Mac were stacking them in place in the barn.

"Cal Baxter!" she exclaimed, standing in the entrance to the barn, her hands on her small waist. Her tone more than the words was a call to attention. Something clearly had her dander up.

"Hi, baby. What's up?"

"Cal, I am going to kill you!" she raged, not moving.

"Well, baby, you picked a great place. There'll be lots of witnesses to your crime," he assured her, taking in his friends' amused looks. "Excuse us, guys, but I think Jess needs to talk to me in private."

"Spoilsport," Tuck called with a laugh.

"I don't mind having this discussion in front of them. After all, they've been involved," she stormed at him, her chin in the air.

He shook his head. "No, thanks. We'll go outside." He took her arm and led her outside and around to the side of the barn before he asked, "What have I done this time?"

"As if you don't know! I asked you not to encourage any of those guys."

"I didn't," he protested. "I mean, I haven't." His gaze roved her body as she stared at him fiercely. Her hair was twisted into one long braid, but small dark wisps had pulled loose to dance around her oval face. Her cheeks were flushed and her green eyes sparked with anger.

"Then why are they still calling me, following me when I go out? Suggesting I should consider marrying them?" She reached out and poked her finger into his chest. "It smacks of your shenanigans, Cal."

"Well, you're wrong. I got the message. I haven't even talked to any of those guys, much less seen them, since we saw Richard at the restaurant."

After glaring at him, she turned and began to pace back and forth in front of him. "If that's true, then I don't understand why they haven't given up. I even got a call or two from some other men not on the list. Like suddenly it's open season on me."

Cal cleared his throat. "Maybe word got out that I was, uh, encouraging others to...you know, get friendly."

Jessica sagged against the barn wall. "I think I didn't appreciate the protection you've given me in the past. I can't get anything done with all these interruptions. I'm going crazy!"

He stepped closer and brushed back a sprig of her hair, his fingers trailing across her flushed cheek. "What can I do to help?"

She gave him a halfhearted smile. "I don't know of anything that can be done. I guess they'll give up eventually."

He hated her sounding so down. At least, he told himself, that's why he came up with his next suggestion. He knew for sure it would work. "There's one way to stop all of it at once."

Surprised, she stared at him. "I don't see how."

"It's simple. We get engaged."

JESSICA'S GREEN EYES widened and she stared at him as if he'd suggested she leap off a cliff. "You're kidding."

"Nope. It would work. It's what half the town has been expecting all along. Everyone would believe it immediately, and none of those guys would dare bother you."

She was having difficulty believing her ears. Her greatest wish in the world was being handed to her. She wanted to pinch herself to see if she was dreaming. "Y-you want to marry *me?*"

Reality returned. He backtracked, stomping on her hopes and dreams.

"Pretend. We'd be pretending until you got your restaurant launched. Then we could break it off, tell everyone we're too close to marry."

"'Too close to marry,'" she repeated, with no inflection. Her heart was breaking. But she couldn't let Cal see how distressed she was.

He straightened and shrugged his shoulders. "It's just a suggestion. After all, I helped cause the problem."

She turned away from him, her arms wrapped around her middle. How should she respond? Could she pretend to love him while hiding that she loved him? Was this her only chance to get Cal to see her as a woman? Could she do anything but agree? No.

"All right," she suddenly responded, turning to face him.

"All right?" he repeated faintly.

She wondered if he was about to pass out. Maybe he hadn't expected her to accept. "Unless you didn't mean it."

"I meant it," he hurriedly assured her.

"Okay."

They stood there, staring at each other, but Jessica didn't know what to say or do. Suddenly she was engaged to Cal, the man she now realized she'd loved since she first met him twenty-three years ago, when he was eight and she was four.

"Uh, what do we do next?" she asked.

"Well, I reckon we need to buy a ring."

"Buy a ring? But it's not…not real."

"If it's going to work, it has to be real for however long it lasts. And going to Mr. Anderson's store and buying a ring will announce it to the entire town. You know how quick the gossip chain is."

"All right, but I'll pay for the ring." She felt guilty enough luring him into the engagement. She didn't want him to be out a lot of money, too.

He seemed to take exception to her thinking, taking her shoulders again and giving her a little shake. "Don't be ridiculous. *I* buy the ring."

"O-okay."

He nodded, seemingly pleased with her agreement. He stared down at her mouth, as if he'd lost track of what the next move should be. All she could think about was wishing he'd kiss her.

When he didn't, she asked, "When? When should we go?"

"Go?" he asked, leaning toward her.

"Go buy the ring. You know, like you said. When should we go to Mr. Anderson's store and buy the ring?"

He stepped back, breaking the intimate moment. "Oh, right. Uh, let me see." He closed his eyes, as if to concentrate. Then he opened them and said, "Let me check with the guys."

"Are you going to tell them?" she asked, suddenly breathless. Telling his friends would make the engagement seem real.

"Not yet. Let's get the ring first."

Her heart sank. Maybe he didn't really mean it. Maybe he intended to keep the engagement quiet. But logic gave her spirits a lift. Keeping it secret wouldn't work.

She followed him to the front door of the barn.

"Uh, guys, I need to run an errand with Jess. Can you manage without me for half an hour?"

"What?" Tuck complained. "You're going to leave us here doing your dirty work while you go play with Jessica?"

"Half an hour?" Jessica echoed at almost the same time.

"Do you think it will take longer?" he asked, surprised.

"I just— Of course not. We might even be able to finish in fifteen minutes if you're fast!" She spun around and headed for her car.

Mac leaned on his pitchfork. "Whatever it is, you'd better plan on a little longer. Jessica doesn't seem happy with you. We'll cover things here."

"Right. I'll check in with you later on." Cal hurried after Jessica.

BY THE TIME Cal caught up with Jessica, she was prepared to drive off. He threw himself into the passenger seat of her car, glaring at her. She'd counseled herself to be calm. If she could. After all, it wasn't every day that a lady got engaged. Especially to the man she'd loved for twenty-three years.

"Are you upset, baby? Did I do something wrong?" Cal asked.

"No, of course not. I know you're busy."

He caught her arm even as she backed out of his driveway. "Hey, you know I always have time for you. Did I not allow enough time for you to choose the ring you like?"

She felt like a shrew. "I'm sorry, Cal. I don't know what I was thinking. I think I'm a little off balance."

Leaning over, he surprised her by dropping a brief kiss on her lips, leaving her wanting more. "Me, too. Come on, let's get this over with."

She pressed her lips together, warning herself not to complain again because he was treating this momentous occasion as if he were shopping for a can of soda.

Momentous occasion? There was her first mistake. No one should call a pretend engagement important. But it was to her. It might be the closest she ever came to achieving her dream.

Since Mr. Anderson's jewelry store was on the town square, a few storefronts down from the sheriff's office, it didn't take long to reach their goal, leaving Jessica little time to reconsider her agreement to Cal's offer.

"Howdy, Sheriff. Jessica. How are you doing today?" Mr. Anderson greeted them. He'd been the only jeweler in town since before their births. In fact, Ed Baxter had bought the modest ring he'd given Mabel from George Anderson.

"Afternoon, Mr. Anderson," Cal replied, and slipped his arm around Jessica, surprising her.

She nodded, trying to smile as if nothing had changed.

When neither she nor Cal added any words to their initial greeting, George Anderson frowned and asked, "Are you needing a plaque for some award or something, Sheriff?"

"Nope. We need a ring."

Jessica, after seeing Mr. Anderson's surprise, looked away.

"Is it your birthday, Jessica?" Mr. Anderson asked, still not quite clear.

"No." She felt irritated that her voice came out in a whisper. Clearing her throat, she looked at Cal.

He seemed taken aback by Mr. Anderson's lack of comprehension. "A *ring,* Mr. Anderson."

"That's what you said, Sheriff. A birthstone? When were you born, Jessica?"

"No, not a birthstone! An engagement ring!" Cal snapped, as if his patience had completely disappeared. The two ladies on the other side of the small shop had no problem hearing him.

After a startled gasp, the women immediately gave up their shopping and rushed for the door.

"An engagement ring? For the two of you?" George Anderson exclaimed, a broad smile breaking across his face.

"Yes," Cal said firmly, bringing his voice back under control. "Do you have something nice?"

"You bet I do. I have just the thing." The elderly man hustled to his office.

Jessica stood rigidly beside Cal, afraid to speak. If

she opened her mouth, she might begin laughing hysterically.

Mr. Anderson quickly returned with a large black velvet box. "These are my special rings. A little pricey, but you can afford it, can't you, Cal?"

Cal stiffened at Mr. Anderson's laugh, his arm tightening around Jessica. "Yes, I can."

"I really don't need a big ring…" Jessica began.

"Let's see them, Mr. Anderson," Cal prompted, ignoring her words.

Was the dratted man intent on getting back to work? Had she taken too much of his precious time? Just as her rage began to rise, she watched him bend over the now open box where six large rings glistened under the artificial light. Cal was taking his time, examining each ring.

"Cal, these are much too large," she whispered.

"Which do you like best?" he asked, sliding the box closer to her. As she bent over the rings, he said to Mr. Anderson, "I know it's unusual, but I'd like something with an emerald in it." Then he added, "For her eyes."

Jessica couldn't believe such a romantic thought had come from Cal. Stunned, she stared at him until Mr. Anderson, having made another trip to his office, brought out a second box. He lifted out a ring consisting of an oval emerald surrounded by large diamonds and showed it to Cal.

"Like this one?"

"Perfect," Cal agreed, taking it from him. He turned to Jessica. "What do you think? Do you like it?"

She took one look at it and fell in love. Though

she had the money now to buy nice jewelry, she hadn't because she was always working in the kitchen. She'd never even looked at a ring like this one. "It's...it's beautiful, but—"

"Give me your finger."

Reluctantly, she surrendered her hand to Cal's. When he slid the slender ring on her third finger, she almost stopped breathing. "Oh."

"Perfect," Cal muttered, staring at the ring. Then he lifted her finger to his lips.

She gasped, unprepared for his action. But there was more to come. He swept her into his arms and kissed her as if he'd never let her go. A kiss she'd always dreamed of, longed for. In Cal's arms, Jessica felt safe and excited, loved and supported. As if she could do anything she wanted because she had Cal by her side. Vaguely, she heard the bell over the door ring, but it didn't seem important at the time.

"What's going on here?" Edith Hauk asked.

Cal released Jessica but said nothing.

It was Mr. Anderson who explained the situation. "Isn't it wonderful? These two just got engaged."

"Oh! Well, congratulations. Let me see the ring," Edith said, rushing to them.

"Actually, Jessica hasn't said this is the ring she wants," Cal warned. "Is it?"

His question was directed at Jessica. Reluctantly, she lifted her gaze from the beautiful ring and nodded, unable to speak.

"Wonderful. Is it a good fit?" Mr. Anderson asked. When she nodded again, he turned to Cal. "If you'll come to my office, Cal, we'll discuss price."

Cal followed him, leaving Jessica to Edith Hauk's mercy.

"My goodness, Spence hasn't said a word. Wait till I get hold of that boy, keeping a secret like that from his mama."

"Uh, Spence didn't know. We've k-kept it a secret...from everyone."

"I see. Well, you've certainly had an exciting month, what with selling your restaurants, too. But I heard you were starting another one. Will you still go ahead with it?"

"Oh, yes, of course," Jessica said, but she wondered why she would waste time on a restaurant when she had Cal to— But she didn't. It was a pretense. She'd almost forgotten. She stared down at the ring.

"It's a beautiful ring. And so unusual to have an emerald in it," Edith commented, her gaze following Jessica's.

"Thank you."

The two men returned to join them.

"You ready, Jess?" Cal asked.

She nodded again, not trusting her voice.

"Well, I'm sure word is spreading all over town by now," Edith said. "Everyone will be so excited. When is the wedding?"

"Uh, we haven't set a date yet," Cal replied.

"I bet your mama will be pushing for an early one," Edith returned, her smile not quite as broad as it was.

Jessica and Cal looked at each other, startled.

"Oh, no. Mabel!" Jessica gasped before the two of them sprinted to the door.

Chapter Eleven

"We've got to get there before she hears the news from someone else," Jessica gasped as she ran. "Or she'll never forgive us."

Cal didn't answer, but he ran to the passenger side of her Lexus. She unlocked the doors and in no time they were racing down the main street of Cactus.

"Careful, or Pete will give you a ticket," he warned, a grin on his face.

"I'll pay it. But we need to reach Mabel now." She turned the corner before she asked the most important question. "We are going to tell her the truth, aren't we?"

Cal didn't respond.

"Cal? It would be cruel to let her believe—"

"I don't know. I want to tell her the truth, but—"

"We have to."

"What about the guys? Mac, Spence, and Tuck. They were trying to help me find you a husband. Do we tell them, too?"

"I—I suppose so," she muttered, not liking the expanded list.

"Well, see, there's the problem. When you tell people the secret, it leaks out."

"You think the guys would—"

"Not intentionally. Neither would Mom and Dad. But they'll hate lying about it. If anyone realizes we're pretending, then all our work will be for nothing."

She pulled into the drive at the Baxters's. "You mean, we have to keep the secret just between the two of us?"

"I can't help but think that will be best. I'm afraid Mom will be upset about the engagement, so when we break it off, it won't bother her so much."

"Why would she be upset?" Jessica asked, confused.

"She might not think we should marry, since we're almost like brother and sister." He made that remark while he stared straight ahead.

"I am so tired of you saying that, Callum Baxter. We are not related. A lot of people have known their husbands or wives all their lives. Besides, I told you Mabel suggested we marry."

He ignored her comment. "Looks like Mom already knows." He nodded to the front door of the house where Mabel could be seen, a big smile on her face. "Let's go face the music. And smile. You're going to have to do some acting if you're going to convince Mom that you love her baby boy."

Jessica got out of the car and raced to Mabel's outstretched arms. She knew how Mabel felt about her marrying Cal.

"Oh, Jessica, I am so happy," Mabel whispered in her ear as she hugged her. Releasing Jessica, Mabel wrapped her arms around Cal's neck. "It's about time, you big galoot. I didn't think you'd ever wake up!"

"You're not upset?" Cal asked, stepping back to look at his mother.

"You bet I am. I can't believe I had to hear the news from Edith Hauk. Why didn't you tell me?"

"Er, we just decided. I wanted to get a ring right away. We didn't think about how fast the news would travel. Where's Dad?"

"He's at the Western Auto getting new tires put on the car. I called him on his cell phone as soon as I heard." Mabel turned back toward the house. "Come on in. I'm preparing a celebratory dinner for the four of us tonight."

Cal gave Jessica a questioning stare, as if to see if she was free, and she nodded. She wasn't about to hurt Mabel's feelings.

Once they were in the kitchen, seated at the table with glasses of iced tea, Mabel studied her ring, giving it her approval. "Perfect with Jessica's eyes. And unique, just like the two of you. Think of the beautiful babies you'll make," she added, beaming at them.

Cal choked on his tea. Setting it down, he said, "We haven't even set a date yet, Mom. Let's don't jump the gun."

"I have my restaurant to start up, Mabel. It's going to take a lot of time."

"So you should get married first," Mabel intoned. "No point in wasting time."

"We thought it might be better to wait until after I get the restaurant started," Jessica returned. Keeping Mabel in the dark was going to cause a lot of problems.

"But, Jess, darling, when you started your first restaurant, it took almost two years," Mabel exclaimed.

"Mother, don't pressure Jess," Cal ordered. "And forget about that silly bet you ladies made. We're not arranging our wedding for anyone but us."

Mabel turned a bland look on the two of them. "Of course not, dear. I was only thinking of the two of you. Now, you go back to the ranch. Jessica, can you stay, or do you have things to do?"

Jessica wasn't about to be left alone with Mabel until she'd gotten a little more used to their pretense. "I need to drive Cal back to the ranch. He rode with me. What time should I be here for dinner?"

"About six-thirty. Cal, can you pick up Jess on your way?"

"Of course, Mom."

"Good." She turned to Jessica. "If he gets there about six, that'll give you a few minutes to cuddle before you come here."

Jessica gulped back the panic that filled her.

Cal stared at his mother. "Mind your own business, Mom."

Mabel arched her eyebrow at him. "I am. My first grandchild isn't going to make an appearance until you do more than hold hands."

Jessica jumped to her feet before Mabel could get more specific about what she wanted them to do. "We'd better go."

"Yeah. I left the guys doing all my work. I'd better go relieve them," Cal said, rising with her.

"Oh, yes."

"'Bye, Mom, we'll see you at six-thirty."

Jessica was already dreading the evening.

CAL WAS AMAZED at how comfortable he was being engaged to Jessica. After all, he and his three friends had fought the idea of marriage for a lot of years.

But because it was Jessica, he was happy.

When they reached his ranch, she sat silently, waiting for him to get out of the car.

"Uh, Jess, I need to kiss you 'bye."

She turned to stare at him. "But—"

"I think the guys are in the house. They're probably watching us."

"I don't think an officer of the law should behave that way in public," she said stiltedly.

He grinned and shifted closer toward her. "We're in your car on my property. Besides, you don't want me to lose status in front of my friends, do you? Come on, baby, we've kissed before."

Watching her cheeks flush, he swallowed the raging hunger that filled him. He'd be gentle. After all, he didn't want to scare her. Slowly bending his head toward hers, he waited until she acknowledged him, her lips rising to meet his. Then his mouth covered hers and he gave her a gentle kiss.

That's all he intended. But when her lips clung to his, trembling with need, he abandoned such gentlemanly thoughts. He pulled her against him and painted her bottom lip with his tongue, teasing for entry. She never hesitated.

Her arms went around his neck and she lay her head back against his shoulder, making the kiss easier to deepen. Their tongues dueled for dominance and his manhood surged against the jeans he wore.

Hell, he wanted to undress her right here, in broad daylight. The need to touch her skin, to feel her against him, was almost overwhelming. He lifted his mouth, then reslanted it across hers, tasting, tempting, loving.

"Cal!" she whispered, wrenching her mouth away. "We've got to stop."

"I don't know if I can," he muttered, his hands stroking her back, lifting her toward him.

"Cal, it's a pretense, remember? We're not engaged and—"

He hated her reminding him of their agreement. With a sigh, he released her, his hands tingling with the urge to touch her again. "Right."

"We shouldn't spend time alone. It seems we...we react rather violently to each other," she said softly, staring at her hands, now tightly clenched in her lap.

"Yeah," he agreed, clearing his throat. "I wonder why that is." He knew why he reacted the way he did. He just needed to know what was going on in her head.

She didn't give him a clue. "I need to get back home."

"Here's your hat, what's your hurry?" he asked, pulling his Stetson back down on his forehead. Their kiss had knocked it askew.

She didn't respond. Nor did she look at him.

"Okay, okay, I'm going. But I need a goodbye kiss."

Her gaze cut up to his in surprise. "What did you call the kiss a minute ago?"

"Oh, baby, that was a hello kiss if ever there was one," he assured her. Then he leaned forward and only brushed her lips with his and got out of the car in one smooth motion. It was either that or take her to the back seat.

Nodding and touching his Stetson, he strode into his house. His friends were standing in the kitchen, glasses of iced tea in their hands, innocent expressions on their faces.

"Anything exciting going on?" Tuck asked.

"I'd guess you've already heard about my engagement, so, nope, there's no news."

Spence grinned. "We're happy for you, Cal. You and Jess make a perfect couple."

"Thanks. Sorry I abandoned you guys to do the rest of the unloading."

Mac handed him some messages. "We found out why you'd left us when we came inside. The phone's been ringing off the wall. Your mom told us what was going on."

"I would've told you first, but someone saw us in George Anderson's store when I was telling him why we were there. They ran out before we could do anything."

"Hey," Tuck said with a laugh, "we know how the gossips work in Cactus. They've certainly talked about all of us for a lot of years."

"Yeah."

"Congratulations, man," Mac said, his voice ringing with sincerity.

"I wasn't sure you'd feel that way."

"Normally I wouldn't. But you and Jess are special. You've always been meant for each other. When did you decide none of those men on the list would do?"

Cal cleared his throat. No lies here. "I realized I didn't want anyone else to father those children she wanted."

"I'm glad you came to your senses," Mac assured him with a laugh.

Spence, too, was happy for them. "Cal, that's great. I'm glad you didn't tell me earlier and ask me to keep it a secret. This way I can tell my mom I knew nothing."

"Yeah. Well, it's not like we kept it a big secret. We just—I mean, she only said yes today."

"And you got your ring on her finger right away."

"Yep."

"Good thinking."

Tuck looked at all his friends before saying, "Are you sure?"

"Sure that I want to marry Jessica?" Cal asked in surprise. "Yeah, I'm sure. We're talking about Jess."

"I know, but marriage is serious business. We all vowed not to fall into that trap." Tuck's voice was tense, serious.

Cal repeated, "It's Jess. There's no trap."

"No, I guess not. But it's going to change things."

"What will it change?" Mac asked.

"Cal won't be able to hang out anymore."

"Hey, Tuck, we don't hang out all that often," Mac said. "Mostly just Saturdays now. And lots of times, when we do, Jess joins us."

"Yeah. I'm happy for both of you, Cal," Tuck hurriedly assured his friend. "Really, I am."

"Thanks."

"Hey, we've got to have another party!"

"Another party? We've just had two. Why would—"

"To celebrate your engagement, Cal," Tuck explained. "Our mothers will probably arrange something, but if they don't, then we will."

"Yeah, okay."

"When's the wedding?" Spence asked.

"We're going to wait until after Jess gets her restaurant up and running."

"Man, you really know how to torture yourself, don't you? Unless you and Jess have already— I mean, it's none of my business but... Never mind." Tuck abruptly ended what he'd been trying to say.

Cal didn't have any difficulty understanding Tuck. If he wasn't going to sleep with Jess before the ceremony, then a quick marriage would be wise.

Grimacing, Cal reminded himself that Tuck didn't know just how much torture he'd volunteered himself for. No sex. Just a few kisses in public.

Enough to get him all hot and bothered, even just thinking about those kisses. He ran his finger inside his shirt collar, hoping to ease the steam that seemed to be rising from him.

"You hot?" Mac asked, watching him.

"Nope." He smiled, trying to distract himself. "You guys should be hot, doing all the work."

"It was half done before you left. And we'd do more than that for you and Jess to be happy," Spence said.

Cal smiled at his friends. "You're the best. I don't know what I'd do without the three of you."

Tuck grinned. "You'd still be out there unloading hay, that's what you'd do."

"Right," Cal agreed with a laugh. Then he'd have an excuse for being all hot and bothered.

IF JESSICA THOUGHT her time had been consumed by certain men calling and pursuing her, it was nothing compared to her afternoon after becoming engaged. Everyone in town called. Or, at least, it seemed like it.

Each one wanted her to tell every detail of her engagement and to describe her engagement ring. They all asked when the wedding would take place, and asked when the engagement party invitations would be sent out. Several offered to host showers for her, asking her to start on a guest list as soon as possible.

She finally turned off her phone and got in the shower, hoping to calm down before Cal came to pick her up for dinner. She wanted to be sure she was ready to go when he got there. It wouldn't do for them to spend much time alone in her town house.

She shuddered as she stood under the warm shower. Just the thought of Cal's hands on her brought shivers to her. How far would he take the pretend engagement? She'd loved him forever, but the sexual element of the relationship was new. She wasn't sure what he would do.

Or what she wanted him to do.

That was the scary part. Today, in the car, she'd

stopped him only because it was during the day. They might have been seen. She'd longed for Cal for so long, she wasn't sure she'd have the strength to resist if he wanted to love her.

As she stepped out of the shower, she heard her doorbell ring. She wrapped her hair in a towel and pulled on a green silk wrapper before she hurried down the stairs, hoping and praying it wasn't Cal.

She swung open the door to a short man whose face was almost hidden by a large vase of a dozen red roses.

"Ms. Hoya?"

"Yes," she said breathlessly, unable to believe that Cal had been so romantic. But she remembered the kiss on her ring. Maybe he was more romantic than she thought.

"Flowers, ma'am," the man said, shoving the vase into Jessica's hands.

"Oh, thank you," she said as she set the flowers on the entry table and found her purse to tip the deliveryman. As soon as she closed the door behind him, she searched for the pristine white card pinned to the ribbon around the vase.

Welcome to our family.
You're already in our hearts.

Mabel and Ed

Even though the roses weren't from Cal, the message brought tears to Jessica's eyes. What wonderful people. Ed and Mabel had been her family ever since her mother's death. The only person she loved more in the world was their son.

After sniffing the perfume of the roses, she hurried back upstairs. Cal could be here any minute.

She was ready when he arrived, only a few minutes before six-thirty. Obviously he'd realized too much time alone would be a problem. She opened the door, ready to step outside.

"Evenin', baby. Aren't you going to ask me in?"

"I thought we should hurry. I don't want to be late."

Instead of looking at her, Cal gazed over her shoulder. "Nice flowers."

"Yes, they're beautiful."

"Who sent them?"

You'd think he was conducting an investigation. Irritated, Jessica raised her brows. "I assumed they would be from you. But I was wrong."

"Sorry. I had a lot to do this afternoon. I didn't think of sending flowers." His voice was stiff until he saw her roll her eyes. "Okay, I wouldn't have thought of sending flowers anyway, but I've never gotten engaged before."

"Me, neither," she reminded him, and pulled the door closed behind her.

"So, really, who are they from?"

He followed her around his truck and held open the door for her. Today she was dressed in a soft denim skirt that made it easy to climb into the high seat. "Jealous?" she asked as she settled in and waited for him to close the door.

He reached up to cup her neck and pulled her face lower so he could kiss her. As his warmth invaded her, Jessica was glad they weren't still in the house. The bed upstairs would be too tempting.

When he pulled back, he asked again, "Who are they from?" She hesitated and he added, "Hell, yes, I'm jealous. You're engaged to me. I won't have some other man sending you flowers."

"Even your father?" she whispered, and dropped another kiss, a brief one, on his tight lips.

"Dad?" he replied, his voice rising. "Dad sent you red roses?"

"Well, actually, they're from Mabel and Ed, to welcome me to the family."

"You little witch, teasing me like that."

"You deserve it. My day has been a disaster, worse than before."

"Men have been calling you?"

"No, but every woman in town wants to hear all about our big romance, and the engagement, and the wedding, and they're offering to give showers and—"

"Whoa! Didn't you tell them we hadn't set a date?"

"I tried. They insisted you were too much of a man to wait that long."

Cal groaned, and Jessica knew just how he felt. She wasn't sure she could wait that long, except that there would be no wedding at the end of her wait.

"Come on, Cal, we're going to be late."

He stared at her, not moving, and her heart raced, wondering what he would do next.

"Well, now, I think I'd better kiss you one more time before we go to my parents'. If you don't look thoroughly kissed, I think Mom will send us back outside. By then, it will be dark, and who knows how I'll contain myself."

He was right. And the real danger was when he brought her home tonight. She'd have to be sure she kept her distance then.

"Okay," she agreed, which surprised him. "You can kiss me now, but not when you bring me home."

He considered her words, then nodded, as if he agreed with her thoughts. "Okay. But this kiss had better be a good one."

She slid down from the high seat, her arms going around his neck, her body pressing against his, and she gave him the kiss of his life.

She arrived at Mabel's looking thoroughly kissed.

Chapter Twelve

After their private celebration with Ed and Mabel, Jessica assumed her life would settle down.

Wrong.

Early the next morning, the phone began ringing again, more friends or neighbors, or gossips, wanting the lowdown on their romance.

Melanie Rule called and offered to host a shower.

"Oh, Melanie, that's so nice of you, but we're not setting a date yet."

"Is Cal wary about getting married?" she asked. "Oh, I don't mean that as a slam against you, Jessica. But you know those four guys have long protested against marriage."

"You're right. But we just thought it would be better to wait. My new restaurant is going to take a lot of time."

"Your new restaurant? You're still going to start another one?"

"Yes, a steak house."

"Wow. If there are any new jobs going, I'd be interested."

"I thought you were happy at the drugstore."

"I meant a night job. I'd like to make some extra money."

Jessica immediately knew where she'd like to have Melanie. She was skillful at dealing with the drugstore customers. "I could use you as hostess in the evenings, if you think you wouldn't be too tired after working all day."

"No, I'd be fine. That would be great. Let me know, okay?" She added, "And when you set the date for the wedding, we'll plan a shower."

"Thanks, Melanie."

Jessica really appreciated Melanie's call. But the rest of them were bothersome. Every time she came up with a new idea, a call would interrupt her concentration.

Finally, in frustration, she turned off the ringer on her phone and left the answering machine to deal with the callers.

Sitting at the kitchen table, she couldn't hear the answering machine in her bedroom upstairs. At last, she had peace and quiet for her work.

CAL ARRIVED AT WORK that morning with a smile on his face.

He liked being engaged to Jessica. He liked thinking about holding her in his arms. He liked the thought of making babies with her.

In fact, he amazed himself. The idea of marriage had never interested him until now. Maybe it was because he hadn't let himself think of marrying Jessica. And no one else seemed right.

But Jessica was the right woman for him.

And he intended to make sure the fake engagement led to a real marriage. Then he could spend the rest of his life with Jessica.

The past and the future coming full circle.

And that thought made him smile even more.

His staff teased him quite a bit that morning. All of them but the new guy, Pete, were married. Each of them came up with some unique advice. They were all laughing over the last piece of advice when the phone rang.

Betty handled the call, and it became apparent to everyone that it was serious. She immediately passed it on to Cal.

"Sheriff Baxter, this is the FBI—Agent Colbrook in Dallas."

"Yes, sir. How can I help you?"

"We have two dangerous criminals we believe are heading in your direction. They're involved in a string of robberies and carjackings in Dallas, one of which ended in a fatality. We're alerting all the law enforcement agencies in the Panhandle that these men may be heading your way. We're going to fax their pictures and information right now."

"Thanks for the info. We'll be alert."

Cal crossed to the fax machine, taking the pages as they began to appear. "Betty, call up Ricky and Pete, let them know what we have here. They need to be alert if they pull someone over. The FBI thinks they're driving a stolen pickup."

He handed the pages over to Betty so that his men out working the county wouldn't be caught unawares.

"And you tell them to put on those bulletproof

vests before they even think of getting out of their vehicles.''

Then he organized the rest of his staff, except for one who was to maintain the office, asking them to cover the different roads that led from Lubbock to New Mexico. He himself took the road that headed southwest, toward Mexico.

Betty stopped Cal as he was about to leave. ''Where's *your* vest?''

''I think it's in the Jeep,'' he muttered, checking the rifle he'd taken from the wall.

Betty circled him and entered his office. Thirty seconds later she returned, holding it out. ''You left it in the closet.''

Cal grimaced. The new jackets were lightweight, but he still didn't like wearing them. ''Thanks, Betty.''

''You promise to wear it. Otherwise, your deputies won't, either.''

He shrugged into it, nodding in agreement. ''Right, as usual. Pass on anything suspicious.''

''Will do.''

Cal left the office with another smile, this one for Betty. She was a mother hen, with all her hovering over the men, but she was a good woman.

Several hours later everything seemed quiet in their county. None of his men had reported any suspicious activity. His mind was dwelling on seeing Jessica again as he drove slowly back toward Cactus.

About five miles out of town, a car sped past him heading in the other direction. It wasn't a truck, but Cal figured even if it wasn't the bad guys, it would be someone who needed to think about their driving habits.

He made a U-turn and stuck the magnetized flashing red light on his roof. Then he pressed down on the gas. It was going to require some speed to catch up. He picked up the microphone and called in to Betty.

"Betty, I'm after a low-flyer, a blue Buick, looks like two men, heading south on County Road 19."

"Cal, you be careful. I just got a report that they found the abandoned truck in Lubbock."

He considered that information. "Find out who's closest and send a backup."

As he gained on them, thanks to the new motor in his old Jeep, Cal picked up the rifle lying on the seat. These men weren't interested in stopping.

He pulled even with the car and motioned the driver to pull over. When he caught the gleam of metal, he ducked and eased up on the gas. Bullets pierced his windshield, shattering the glass. Cal put the rifle out the left window, braced it against his Jeep and fired several rounds, hoping to get lucky.

He must've been living right, because one of his bullets caught the Buick's back left tire. As the driver fought to control the car, the other man discharged more bullets.

Cal came to a halt a few yards behind them and scooted across the front seat of the Jeep to open the passenger door. "Come out with your hands up," he yelled.

"Yeah, right!" the passenger snarled, and came out of the car with two guns pointed at Cal. He began firing from both guns. Cal jumped back in the Jeep, knowing the door wouldn't be much of a shield.

The man ran forward and sent several bullets into the vehicle as Cal fired back.

And that was the last he knew.

JESSICA WAS ENJOYING a cup of hot tea, reviewing her notes, humming along to a country-western song on the radio. Music soothed her.

"We interrupt our programming with a special bulletin. A local sheriff has been shot while attempting to apprehend two murder and armed robbery suspects. Sheriff Cal Baxter of Cactus has been taken to County Hospital. No word yet on his condition. We'll update our information as soon as it's available."

Jessica stared at the radio as if it had sprouted horns. She couldn't believe what she'd just heard. Cal wasn't in danger. They never had serious crime in Cactus. The information couldn't be true. She must've imagined it. Why hadn't anyone called her if Cal was in trouble?

Then she remembered turning off her phone. She raced upstairs and pushed Play on her answering machine, hitting the skip button when she recognized another lazy, happy drawl.

Then Mabel's tense voice came out of the machine. "Jess, Cal's been shot, they're taking him to—"

Jessica never heard the rest of the message. She tumbled down the stairs, grabbed her purse and keys from the kitchen cabinet, and raced to her car.

"Dear God, please let him be all right! Please!"

How could this happen? Cactus was a quiet, peaceful town. What had gone wrong?

She drove like a maniac to the hospital, abandoning her car, keys still in it, near the emergency entrance.

"Hey, lady, you can't park there," a security guard called.

She ignored him and kept running for the automatic door to the emergency room. She vaguely recognized the nurse behind the desk as someone she'd known in school, but it didn't matter. "Cal? Where—"

The nurse pointed down a hall behind her position, her eyes wide.

Jessica raced in that direction, her gaze frantically darting back and forth to the rooms that lined the hall. Someone in uniform stepped out of the last cubicle.

"Jessica, he's all right," Ricky, one of the deputies, hurriedly said.

"All right? They said he was shot!" she screamed, staring at him incomprehensively.

Her response alerted Ed and Mabel and Betty, who stepped past the curtain together and came to meet Jessica.

She took Mabel's hands, trying to control her sobbing. "Cal! Is he really all right? Where is he? What happened?"

"Jess?" Cal called from the cubicle.

She didn't wait for answers to her questions. She darted past the curtain, then came to an abrupt halt.

Cal was sitting up on the bed, his shirt off, while a doctor was working on his left arm.

"Cal?" Jessica called, her voice wobbling. "Are you all right?"

He held out his right arm and she ducked into his embrace.

"Steady, there," the doctor ordered.

"What's he doing?" she demanded, her voice cracking, her body shaking.

"I got nicked and he's sewing me up."

One of the other deputies stepped up. "Cal's lucky Betty made him wear his bulletproof vest, or he'd be dead right now."

Jessica turned around, spying Cal's receptionist who had followed her back into the cubicle. "Bless you, Betty."

"Still left a big bruise," Ed muttered.

Jessica turned her attention back to Cal, smoothing her hands over his bare chest. He winced, and she pulled her hands back as if she'd touched fire.

"Easy, baby. I'm a little sore."

She stared at him. Then she completely lost it. Bursting into tears, she leaned into his neck, sobbing with relief that Cal was still the center of her world.

CAL DIDN'T NEED ANYONE to tell him he'd been lucky. If one of his bullets hadn't struck the man with the guns, he'd definitely have come out worse, if not dead. Then, if several of his men, flying down the road, their sirens blaring, hadn't scared the other man, who'd taken off running, he probably would've completed the job his fallen friend had tried to do.

Yep, he'd been lucky.

Of course, when he awoke the next morning, in a spare bedroom in his parents' house, he didn't feel quite so lucky. He ached all over, but his arm and chest in particular were painful.

The doctor had prescribed pain pills. He vaguely remembered Jessica giving him one last night. Then he didn't remember anything.

He groaned as he took a deep breath. That hurt.

"Cal? Are you awake? Do you need something?"

Jessica popped up, and Cal realized she'd slept beside him on the king-size bed. Damn, the first time she'd slept with him and he couldn't remember it.

"What are you doing in here?" he asked, surprised to hear his voice slur. He hoped her presence meant she'd realized how right they were for each other. How real their engagement should be. He'd been encouraged by her reaction yesterday at the hospital.

"I'm taking care of you, just like I always have. Remember when you broke your arm?"

He sighed. Just like always. He guessed she'd been afraid of losing a friend yesterday, instead of a lover. At least he had their friendship as a starting point.

Staring at her, he decided she looked as if she needed care, instead of him. Dark circles were under her eyes and her hand trembled as it rested on his good arm. "Did I keep you up half the night?"

"No, you scarcely moved."

"Then why do you look like you haven't slept in a month, baby?"

Instead of answering him, she slipped off the other side of the bed and crossed the room to the bathroom. He noticed she was dressed in the same jeans and T-shirt she'd worn yesterday.

"Jess?" he called after her.

She reappeared almost immediately. "Sorry. I didn't realize I looked so bad. I'll go—"

"No! Hell, baby, I don't care if you don't look your best. I was just concerned about you." He lifted his right arm toward her.

She took his hand. "I didn't sleep well."

"Probably 'cause I didn't kiss you good-night," he teased, hoping to see a smile on her lips.

No such luck. Instead, they trembled.

"Baby, what's wrong?"

"What's wrong? What's wrong? You could've died, Cal! That's what's wrong."

"But, Jess, I didn't. I'm too stubborn to—"

Before he could finish, a knock sounded on the door.

Mabel opened the door. "Is everything all right?"

Jessica stood rigid beside the bed, seemingly unable to speak. Cal looked at his mom. "I was concerned about how tired Jess looked."

Come to think of it, his mother didn't look a lot better.

"I guess I caused y'all a lot of worry, but, really, I'm fine," he assured them, then winced as he tried to shift on the bed.

"I think he needs another pain pill," Jessica said at once.

"I'll bring up his breakfast," Mabel added, and both women started to leave him.

"Wait a minute! Don't I get a say in anything? I don't want a pain pill. It knocked me out last night and I don't want to lose consciousness again. And I'll come down for breakfast as soon as I shower, Mom."

Mabel looked at him doubtfully.

Jessica, however, wasn't as willing to let him have his way. "The pain pills for this morning aren't as strong as last night. The doctor said you'd get well faster if you take them, because it will relax the muscles."

Her chin was up, a sure sign of her stubbornness. Cal grinned. "You promise it won't make me pass out?"

She nodded.

"Okay, I'll take a pill after I eat. Mom, give me five minutes for a shower."

Jessica intervened again. "No shower. You'll have to take a bath because you can't get your stitches wet."

"Damn. I think I'll go back to sleep and wake up another day. Maybe everything will be better then." He frowned at Jessica.

For the first time, a small smile peeked out. "Your choice. I have a pill for that, too."

Mabel laughed. "I see everything's under control here. I'll go start his breakfast. And yours, too, Jess."

"Oh, no, Mabel that's not—"

"Yes, it is necessary," Cal said firmly, staring at her. "You're going to need your energy to take care of me."

"I won't argue about that," Jessica agreed.

But her smile remained in place, indicating she didn't mind taking care of him, and that made Cal happy.

Jessica decided Cal didn't seem quite as happy when, after his mother left, he tried to throw back the covers and rise.

The doctor had warned her and Mabel that Cal would have considerable stiffness and pain. She pulled the covers back farther, trying to ignore the picture of Cal in his white briefs, stretched out on the bed.

"Take it slowly, Cal. The doctor said—"

"I don't care what the damned doctor said. This hurts!"

"That's exactly what he said."

"Thanks."

She grinned at his sarcastic response. At least he sounded normal. She'd been so shaken last night and this morning at the thought of losing Cal, it was reassuring to hear him complain.

As he tried to sit up, she slid an arm behind his back and lifted as much as she could. He was a big man. There was no way she could lift him by herself.

As soon as he was upright, sweat breaking out on his brow, she lifted his legs to the floor.

"Hey, there's nothing wrong with my legs!"

"I was just trying to conserve your strength. The doctor said you should take it easy at first." She watched his jaw square and his lips press together. Cal Baxter was known for his hardheadedness.

Maybe that was why he'd never married.

Dismissing that thought, she wrapped her arm around his waist as soon as he was standing. She certainly didn't want to chance his falling. If there was anything he didn't need, it was more bruises.

He laid his arm around her shoulders and they made slow progress to the connecting bath. She helped him sit on the closed commode so she could run his bathwater.

As she adjusted the temperature of the water, he said, "I want to know just how far your nursing is going to go." His breathing had evened out after the strenuous walk to the bathroom. "Are you going to bathe me?"

She gave him a mock look of shock. "Of course not."

"Why not? It wouldn't be the first time you've seen me naked."

With his gaze on her, she felt her cheeks heat. "But that was over twenty years ago when you taught me about skinny-dipping. And both our mothers made it clear why we'd better not do *that* again."

He smiled. "Yeah, but we're all grown up now. The rules are different. Besides, we're engaged."

Jessica gave a cautious look to the door she'd closed behind them. "Behave, Cal. You have to bathe yourself. I'll leave a towel nearby. When you're finished, drain the water, put the towel over you, and I'll come help you get out of the tub."

"I don't think I can manage without a kiss."

Her gaze whipped back to him, catching the teasing glint in his eyes. "This is not the time to play games."

"Baby, I never felt more like playing games in my life. Because I can."

He still had a grin on his lips, but she caught the dark significance of his words. And she couldn't agree more. "Okay," she agreed without argument. "One kiss."

Reaching for her waist, he tipped her into his lap before she knew what was happening. And by the twist of his lips, paid for his behavior with pain.

"Oh, Cal, you'll hurt yourself."

"Yeah, but I think it'll be worth it. Give me my kiss."

Conscious of his near nudity, the warmth of his body, the strength of her wounded warrior, Jessica didn't hesitate to comply with his request.

Besides, it was what she wanted.

Their lips met in a fierce coming together, a draining, life-reinforcing kiss that celebrated what they shared. Immediately Jessica wrapped her arms around his broad shoulders and clung with all the fervor of her being, giving thanks that Cal was alive.

His lips pressed for deeper union, his tongue pulled her into his being, his arms held her against him. She almost became one with him by the kiss alone.

When she felt his burgeoning erection against her legs, she knew they should stop. He certainly wasn't in any condition to carry the embrace to its logical conclusion, but his closeness felt so good, so right, that she only pressed closer.

Until her feet got wet.

Chapter Thirteen

By the time the overflowing bathwater had been mopped, breakfast consumed and Cal returned to his bed, he was ready to admit his need for rest.

Spence and Tuck arrived about the time he subsided onto the mattress. He was glad to see his friends. But Jessica used their arrival as an excuse to leave his side. Though he felt guilty for his selfishness, he wanted her with him.

Mabel, who'd escorted the two visitors to his bedroom, grinned. "She'll be back after she has a shower and packs some clothes, son."

He glared at his mother. Her response made his need clear to his friends. She kept grinning but left the room.

"I hear you scared Jess bad," Spence said. "Us, too."

"It wasn't in my plans. It just happened that way," Cal assured his friends.

"It must've been tough," Tuck added.

"Sort of. But everything happened quickly. And I missed a lot of the action by passing out about the time Ricky and Hank arrived."

"How long you gonna be down?" Spence asked.

"Long enough to miss a rodeo or two," Cal assured him. The thought of those Saturday roughhouses with his friends made him feel old. "Actually, I'll be out of the office for a few days, but that's 'cause the doc is cautious." Dr. Greenfield had delivered all four of them. He was an institution in Cactus.

"Yeah," Tuck murmured. "Remember when I broke my arm playing football? He thought I should stay out the rest of the season."

All three of them laughed since Tuck had played the next game. The door opened on their laughter.

"Well, it seems you're doing better than expected if you can laugh," Mac said from the doorway.

"Come on in, Mac. We were just reminiscing," Cal chuckled.

Mac pulled a chair alongside the other two and settled in. "Well, we've got a few memories, don't we?"

In the general agreement, it was Spence who grew somber. "It makes a fellow think, something like this happening."

"What do you mean?" Tuck growled.

"Facing death, whether it's you or a friend, makes you think about all the things you've done. It might even help us understand our parents' wanting grandchildren."

No one spoke until Tuck looked at Cal. "What do you think, Cal?"

"Hell, I don't have to think. I'm engaged. It's you guys who need to change direction. I'm going to produce some grandchildren as fast as I can."

"And don't he look miserable thinking about doing that producing?" Tuck teased.

Cal laughed with his friends, but his temperature indeed was rising. Every time he thought about making love to Jessica he grew hot.

Mac shook his head. "You guys go ahead and produce the kids. I'll be their doting uncle. That'd be best."

Cal studied his friend. "Don't give up on life yet, Mac," he said softly. "If you'd told me last year I'd be marrying Jess, I'd have thought you were crazy."

Mac smiled. "You would've, but the rest of us always believed you were meant for each other."

"Hey," Spence said, drawing everyone's attention. "Do you see anyone for me?"

"I'm no palm reader, Spence. Find your own woman," Mac returned.

"I bet your mother would help you," Tuck said with a grin.

"Hell, all our mothers are on the warpath, looking for brides. Any hint of a willing woman and you'll be tied up faster than a stray calf," Cal advised his friend.

"Even Aunt Flo is participating in this debacle," Mac said.

"Participating?" Tuck said, staring at Mac. "I heard she's the one who started the entire bet. In fact, if any of us, except for Cal, here, who wants to get married, is trapped, we can lay it at your feet."

"Not me! Aunt Flo's maybe, but not mine."

"Besides," Spence added, "as soon as Cal and Jessica make a baby, the bet will be over, and we'll all be safe."

Interestingly enough, Cal thought he caught a sad note in Spence's voice. Did his friend really want to be married? Had he simply gone along with their sentiment because he was a friend?

"Well, I'll try to rescue you guys as soon as possible."

"It doesn't sound like it if you're postponing the wedding for a couple of years," Mac pointed out.

Cal was suddenly reminded that he was the only member of the new couple who thought they would be married. But that didn't deter him. "It's under negotiation."

"That'a boy," Mac cheered.

"Well, now that you've agreed to rescue all of us from Operation Baby, we'd better let you get some rest. Jessica will be back in a little while and we want you up to snuff for whatever, er, happens."

Cal wasn't enough of an optimist to think that he'd be up to bedroom Olympics today. But he intended to bring that event to fruition as soon as possible.

Because he'd discovered a truth yesterday.

The only thing he would have regretted, had he died yesterday, was not making love to Jessica.

And as soon as he was able, he intended to take care of that omission.

MAC LEFT CAL'S BEDROOM in a melancholy mood. Oh, he was happy for his friend. Cal's love for Jessica was in his eyes. Mac thought they made a perfect couple. If any pair had a chance of happiness, Cal and Jessica did.

He couldn't help remembering, however, when he'd felt as optimistic as Cal. It hadn't lasted. The pain of his divorce was more than he ever wanted to face again.

Maybe he was a coward. He hadn't thought so, but his unwillingness to risk his heart again made him think that maybe he might be.

Well, too bad. He'd cheer for Cal and Jess's marriage, but, coward or no, he wasn't going to risk his own heart ever again.

FOR THE NEXT SEVERAL DAYS, Jessica stayed with Mabel and Ed, providing around-the-clock care for Cal.

Well, not quite around-the-clock. She didn't stay in the same bedroom with him after that first night. And she didn't flood the bathroom again.

But she was at his beck and call. Her restaurant held no interest for her as long as Cal needed her. The thought of living in this world without him rearranged her priorities.

After three days he seemed his old self, scarcely even demonstrating any stiffness. In spite of her protests, he even went back to the office, though he promised to leave any active work to his staff.

After he lustily kissed her goodbye on the fourth morning after his accident, she packed her bags, hugged Mabel and Ed goodbye and returned to her town house.

"What are you doing at home?" Cal barked into the phone when she answered its persistent ringing an hour later.

"Why wouldn't I be at home?"

"You should be at Mom's. I thought you'd stay there."

"Cal, if you're well enough to return to work, you don't need me waiting on you hand and foot." Not that she'd minded. She found sweet pleasure in making him happy.

"I know, but I liked it," he said, and she could hear his grin.

"I bet you did, you rat. Maybe you took advantage of me," she accused, though she wasn't serious.

"No, baby, I wouldn't do that. How about I take tomorrow off and we go for a ride? You've been neglecting Red again."

"Ride? Are you crazy, Cal? You don't need all that jolting around. It's too soon."

"Okay, how about the day after tomorrow? That'll give me another day to rest, but Olé needs the exercise, too. Dad can't ride him, though he'll probably try if I don't do it. You know how determined he is."

"Yes," she agreed with a sigh. "Just like his son." Cal grunted his disapproval of her comparison, but she continued. "Why don't you get one of your friends to exercise the horse. You know they'd be glad to help."

"Yeah, but I want to do it…with you. And I'm sure not going to ask one of my friends to share a ride with you. That's my privilege."

"And one you've exercised many times in the past. It could wait, Cal."

"Day after tomorrow," Cal insisted. "I'll be ready."

"Fine. Be hardheaded. We'll ride on Wednesday," she agreed with a sigh.

"Good. Now, tonight, why don't we go to The Old Cantina for dinner? I'll pick you up at—"

"But, Cal, everyone's going to go crazy, wanting to talk to you—and us. They were still talking about our engagement when you got shot."

"I know. But we need to get it over with. Then maybe they'll leave us alone."

Jessica doubted that. The engagement alone would cause talk for months. Cal and his friends were famous for their stance on marriage.

The bachelors in town were defending their choice to remain unmarried, and the young women were celebrating the capitulation of one of the most eligible. Combining that with Cal's heroic behavior, Jessica figured they'd be the topic of conversation for a long time.

"Okay, but I'll pick you up. You don't need to be driving any more than necessary."

"Sounds good, baby. I love it when you take care of me."

She laughed. "Seems to me you weren't singing the same tune when you had the mumps fifteen years ago."

"That's because you spilled a glass of ice water on me," he reminded her. "That was a real shock to my body. I hope it didn't affect my ability to have children."

"Cal! It didn't. Your mother said—"

"Just teasing, sweetheart," he told her with a chuckle. "I think I can still perform."

Remembering the few times they'd embraced, she was sure he could, too. Just thinking about it made her heart speed up.

"Um, I'll pick you up at six-thirty," she said, hoping to bring the conversation to a close before she dwelled too long on his performance.

He laughed, a reassuring sound. "Right. I'll be ready."

She hung up the phone, thinking about his last words. She'd be ready, too. His accident had changed her thinking about a lot of things. She was ready for whatever Cal wanted.

And, if it involved a seduction, she would volunteer to be the seducer. Maybe it might even turn out the way Mabel wanted. But she wasn't going to live her life without having made love to Cal. His accident had convinced her to agree to whatever he wanted. If he didn't marry her, she'd at least still have memories of lying in his arms.

It reminded her of those old World War Two movies where the man had asked for the woman's love because he might never return. Cal hadn't asked yet. But if he did, she already knew her answer. Or maybe she should do the asking.

Whatever. She'd be ready.

MABEL AND ED ENDED UP going with them to The Old Cantina. Along with half the population of Cactus. Or at least it seemed like it to Jessica.

The restaurant received so many offers to buy their meal, they started a collection. Once Cal was told of the many donations, he designated the money to go to a women's shelter recently established in Cactus to serve the entire county.

Things snowballed from there as the waitresses informed all their customers of the collection. By the end of the evening, close to three hundred dollars had been collected.

"Son," Ed said with pride, "I reckon you could win any election around here, hands down, tonight."

"Too bad the election for sheriff doesn't roll around until next spring," Cal returned with a grin.

"Are you going to run again?" Jessica asked.

Both men stared at her as if she'd lost her mind. Mabel gave her a solemn look but said nothing.

"Of course I will, baby," Cal finally replied. "Why wouldn't I?"

"How about the fact that you were almost killed a few days ago?"

Cal studied her for a minute and then said, "Did you hear about Harriet McGee?"

She stared at him, confused by his non sequitur. What did the town librarian have to do with anything? "No. What about her?"

"She died two days ago. Had a brain aneurism."

"What? I hadn't heard. How terrible," Jessica exclaimed, looking to Mabel for confirmation.

Cal didn't wait for any comments. "Safe job, librarian."

Jessica froze. His point was obvious, and not one she wanted to hear. She stiffened and glared at the love of her life. "That's not—"

"Yes, it is," Cal assured her.

"Your job is more dangerous."

"Want me to quote statistics for you? Do you know how many accidental deaths involved lawmen in this county last year compared to regular people in safe jobs?"

"You don't know those stats by memory," Jessica argued.

"Sure I do. 'Cause it was zero to, um, something over ten."

"What happened to Cal was a rare event," Ed said softly, leaning toward Jessica. "I served for thirty years and never came close to being hurt."

"Except for when you fell into that cactus," Mabel said calmly, continuing to eat her enchiladas.

"Now, Mabel, that don't really count," Ed protested.

They all laughed because Ed's attempt to arrest a man a few years earlier had resulted in the man pushing Ed away, causing him to fall into a cactus. While not lethal, the removal of the cactus spines had been painful.

"Jess," Cal said quietly as the laughter died, "being sheriff is who I am. As much as I love you, I can't change that."

He was pretending in front of his parents, Jessica reminded herself. He wanted them to continue to believe in the engagement, that's all. But, oh, how his words took her breath away. Playing her role wasn't difficult. She loved him with all her heart. "I know," she whispered. "But I want you to be safe."

He leaned over to brush his lips across hers. "I will be, baby. You're stuck with me for the next fifty years."

She stiffened her spine. "Do you think you're getting away that soon, mister?"

"Okay, okay, we'll make it seventy-five, but you're driving a hard bargain, lady. I'll probably have to demand at least four kids to make it worth it.''

Mabel applauded. "I'd love four grandchildren.''

"Now, Mother…'' Ed warned, "don't mess in their business.''

"Oh, Ed Baxter, you know you're just as excited about the grandchildren as I am,'' Mabel argued.

"I wouldn't mind hearing the patter of little feet again,'' Ed admitted. "It sure was fun when Cal was little.'' A reminiscent smile on his face almost brought a tear to Jessica's eye. As a child, the only father figure she'd had was Ed, who had made her feel he loved her almost as much as he did Cal. She wanted that for her children. A father, a grandfather.

Cal smiled at his parents. "I imagine all of us would be happy about that, Dad. Just be patient.''

"Of course, son. The decision is yours and Jessica's.''

Jessica trembled. How disappointed they were going to be when Cal told them the engagement had been a sham and there would be no precious babies.

CAL DIDN'T SEE Jessica the next day. It was the first day he hadn't spent at least some time with Jessica since his accident. He missed her.

He called that evening to reconfirm their riding date. "You haven't forgotten about tomorrow, have you?'' he asked when she answered the phone.

"Tomorrow?'' she asked. "What's tomorrow?''

He could hear the teasing in her voice and played along. "Our ride. Remember?''

"Cal, are you sure you're up to a ride?''

"Oh, yeah, I'm ready for it.'' And a lot more, but

he wasn't going to tell Jessica that now. "Mom is going to pack us a picnic lunch. All you have to do is show up, baby, looking as beautiful as usual."

"Flattery will get you everywhere," she returned in a sultry voice.

"I'm counting on it."

"Seriously, Cal, we probably shouldn't ride long. Aren't you still sore?"

"Don't worry about me. I've ridden since you have. But we'll take it easy. I'll pick you up about ten. Okay?"

"Okay. But I could meet you at the ranch."

"Nope. I'll pick you up. See you tomorrow."

"Okay."

"Baby?" he called softly before she could hang up.

"Yes?"

"You owe me a good-night kiss." Then he hung up the phone.

He hoped she'd forgive him for the plans he'd made. But he couldn't wait any longer.

CAL HAD A PROBLEM.

As sheriff, he was easily recognizable. Any move he made was carefully watched. Especially since his recent notoriety. Having stopped by the office, he put his hands on his hips and surveyed the officers on duty.

"Pete, can I see you a minute?"

The rookie officer jumped. He hadn't enjoyed the lecture Cal had given him a few days ago about being overly zealous in passing out traffic tickets. Cal knew he was worried he'd done something else wrong. He smiled to ease the young man's fears.

Once they were inside the office, Cal ran his finger around the collar of his denim shirt. "Uh, Pete, I need a favor."

Relief filled the young man's face. "Sure, Cal, anything."

Cal rubbed his chin. "This is a personal favor, and you can refuse, if you want." He paused. "I need you to buy me some condoms."

Pete stood still, as if waiting for something else.

"Well?"

"That's it?" the young man asked cautiously.

"Yeah, that's it." When Pete acted as if he didn't understand, Cal added, "Hell, man, everyone knows me. I might as well announce my intentions with a skywriter."

"But...I mean, what do you usually do?"

"I buy 'em in Lubbock. But I don't have time to go today and... Will you do it?" He wasn't going to explain the urgency of his need.

"Well, sure I'll do it, Cal. No problem." The man started out of the office.

"Wait. Here's some money."

"Okay. I'll be right back."

"Great. Don't...don't tell anyone they're for me."

He felt like an idiot. He'd always had this problem.

When his father was sheriff, he knew word would get out if he bought condoms in town. Of course, his father had given him a talk about responsibility, but he hadn't wanted to announce any personal plans to the town.

Betty knocked on his office door. "What are you still doing here? I thought you were taking the day off."

"I'll be gone in a few minutes. Any problems?"

"None that we can't handle. Get yourself out of here before a problem walks in the door."

Cal felt his cheeks heating up. "Not till Pete gets back. He's, uh, running an errand for me."

Betty gave him a knowing look, and Cal felt as if he'd been caught pulling the pigtail of the redheaded girl in the second grade.

"I'll...I'll go through my mail," he muttered, sitting back down behind his desk and reaching for the stack of envelopes in his in-box.

"You do that," Betty agreed with a grin. "I'll send Pete in when he gets back."

"Yeah, thanks."

As soon as the door closed behind him, Cal got up from his desk again. He was too edgy to worry about the mail. He had plans for today, big plans.

A knock sounded on the door.

"Come in."

Pete walked in with a grin on his face. "You didn't say what kind you liked, so I got—" He reached into the brown paper sack and Cal realized he was about to show him what he'd bought. Unfortunately, he'd left the door open and Betty was watching them.

Cal leaned forward and slammed the door. "I don't care what kind. Thanks, Pete."

"Here's your change," he said, holding out his hand.

Cal took it and vowed to drive to Lubbock soon to stock up on, uh, personal purchases.

For today, however, he had what he needed.

Now all he had to do was convince Jess to cooperate.

Chapter Fourteen

Jessica paced the floor of her living room, pausing to stare out the front window. She'd trained herself over the years to get used to not seeing Cal. Amazing how worthless all that training was now that they'd spent some time together.

Frowning, she noticed some clouds. She didn't want anything to spoil their ride. She was looking forward to spending the day with her pretend fiancé.

In fact, she had big plans.

Yesterday she'd gone to the drugstore and made a purchase. She was glad Melanie wasn't there to wait on her. Otherwise, she'd have been embarrassed. But she wasn't going to trap Cal into marriage by an unexpected baby, in spite of Mabel's plans.

But that didn't mean she was going to keep her hands off him. After his accident, she'd realized she was going to make love with him at the first opportunity. And that decision had stayed with her.

In fact, she could think of little else.

Lying in Cal's arms, being one with him, kissing him until her lips were numb with exhaustion, if that could ever happen, were all that filled her mind.

The sound of his truck alerted her to his arrival. Her stomach did a double flip. Okay, their engagement was a pretense, but she wanted some memories for her heart. Memories she would have as she lived out her life alone.

She opened her door, a smile on her lips, hoping Cal wouldn't realize how nervous she was. If he did, he'd want to know what was going on.

He wasted no time.

"I missed you, baby," he said, and swept her into his arms, his lips covering hers.

Oh, yes, she thought, and then she didn't think at all. Her mind was overcome with rapturous sensations, and she enthusiastically cooperated.

"Whoa," Cal finally said, breathing heavily as he set her away from him. "We'd better slow down or those horses aren't going to get any exercise."

Jessica put a smile on her face, but she was a little frustrated. He was more concerned about the horses than making love to her!

Never mind. She was patient.

"Of course. I'm ready." She walked past him to his truck. A neighbor waved to her when she stepped outside. Obviously Cal's kiss was for his benefit. And she'd hoped it was really because he'd missed her.

Cal didn't seem inclined to talk once they were on their way, but Jessica asked about his day at the office and about his mother and father.

"Mom fixed a big lunch. She must think you're underfed," he said. "She made me promise to make sure you ate. Especially dessert."

"Mmm, what kind of dessert?"

"I don't know. She wouldn't tell me."

She had another kind of dessert in mind, but she'd eat some of Mabel's, too. She wouldn't want to hurt her feelings.

When they reached the ranch, she discovered Cal had their two horses already saddled. "I would've saddled my own," she protested.

"Actually, I had Dad come out and help me. It still hurts to lift something heavy," Cal told her. He pushed his Stetson back and grinned at her.

She smiled but worried that her plans were too ambitious today. What if it caused him pain? She took a deep breath. No, it would be all right. If he could ride, he could make love with her.

He loaded the food in two saddlebags and tied one on each saddle.

"Where are we going to picnic?"

"I thought we'd ride to the far side of ranch, near the old line cabin. Remember that big old tree we used to climb?"

"Of course I remember it. I almost fell out of that tree when I was seven."

"That's the one. I thought we'd picnic in its shade."

Jessica looked up at the sky as she absentmindedly stroked Red's nose. "I don't see any sun."

"It is a little cloudy now, but I'm sure it will change later. Did you bring a jacket just in case?"

"No, but my sweater should be warm enough."

"Okay. Let's mount."

Soon they were riding across the pastures, as they had a hundred times over the years. The richness of their past only added to the wealth of their future.

She'd shared so much with Cal. Sharing the ultimate intimacy seemed the only thing to do.

She smiled at him as he turned to look at her. "Are you hurting?"

"A twinge now and then. Nothing important. Of course, my chest looks like someone painted it with yellow paint from kindergarten."

"Is it still sore to the touch?"

"I don't know. Betty doesn't stroke my chest much."

She sent him an exaggerated look. "I should hope not."

He continued as if she hadn't spoken. "And my fiancée has been ignoring me."

"Really? I heard she'd taken good care of you."

He reached out and pulled Red to a stop alongside Olé. Then he leaned over and kissed her. "I think you're right."

"Thank you. And for agreeing, said fiancée will do a little stroking after lunch."

"After lunch?"

She nodded, noticing his sparkling eyes, their gray suddenly appearing silver.

"You know," he said, "I feel hungry all of a sudden. Let's have our picnic here."

She laughed and took her reins again, urging Red forward. "I don't think so. You promised me our favorite tree."

But she was growing more optimistic about her plans. She didn't think she'd have to work too hard at persuading Cal to make love.

CAL'S PULSE WAS RACING.

All he could think about was making love to Jessica. He didn't intend to let anything stop him today. It was time to take their friendship to another level.

"How are your parents doing?" Jessica asked. "Have they recovered from your accident?"

He looked at her sharply. "You heard them at dinner the other night. They understand." After a pause, he asked the difficult question. "Do you?"

"I suppose." She shot him a glance out of the corner of her eye. "You said it was a rare occurrence."

"It is. Besides, I don't try to run your business."

"You told me I wouldn't have time for marriage and a restaurant."

He'd forgotten those rash words. "I was trying to encourage you to keep thinking about marriage. You're the one who seemed to think it was one or the other. Do you still?"

She leaned forward to stroke Red's neck, then sat back up with a sigh. "I don't know. I couldn't manage a lot of restaurants and have a family, but I don't think I'd want a chain of restaurants again. I could manage one restaurant, as long as my...husband was flexible and helpful."

"Hmm, a flexible husband. I haven't heard of that variety," he teased.

"Me, neither, but I think it's up to the wife to train him."

"Train? You make him sound like a puppy."

She smiled and reached over to touch his arm. "No. But I believe both members of a marriage should communicate their needs and wants. I'm not into martyrdom, like some women."

"Good. 'Cause if I get married, I want to know what makes my wife happy." He hoped his plans for the afternoon would make his future wife happy. It was something he'd want to do over and over again.

He grinned at his thoughts, and Jessica raised an eyebrow in question. He shook his head and pressed his heels into Olé's side for a little more speed. He didn't want to wait any longer to feel her against him.

He could barely guide his horse, he was so busy watching Jessica. Her rear lovingly molded in her tight jeans, her breasts moving up and down. How he longed to cup them in his hands, feel their fullness. His body stirred even more, making him uncomfortable.

Damn, this ride was longer than he remembered!

Finally, they were approaching the tree they'd played in as children. Its low, wide branches had been perfect for their adventures.

He hoped his plans for today were going to work out. The package Pete had bought for him was in his hip pocket. He'd thought about slipping it into the saddlebags and letting Jessica find it, but he was afraid she'd be too shocked.

But life was too short to put off loving Jessica.

Just as they rode up the rise toward the tree, he heard the rumble of thunder. A quick look at the gathering black clouds told him he'd been preoccupied and hadn't seen the storm approaching. They were going to have to adjust their plans.

"Jess, we're going to have to take shelter. Head for the line cabin," he ordered quickly.

She took a look at the sky and nodded in agreement, urging Red toward the old shack. Cal's father and the neighboring rancher had built it together thirty years ago, for just such instances as this.

They didn't make it in time. The rain started pouring down in sheets, and when they reached the cabin they were soaked to the skin. Cal grabbed Red's reins as Jessica swung out of the saddle.

"Get inside," he yelled over the noise of the storm. "I'll take care of the horses."

There was a shelter behind the cabin for animals. He took both horses there and pulled their saddles off, using the saddle blankets to rub them down. Then he grabbed the saddlebags and dashed for the cabin.

Jessica had been watching for him and swung the door open as he arrived. Inside the cabin, he dropped the saddlebags on the rough-hewn table and shook himself.

"Wow. So much for the sunshine," he said to Jessica.

She smiled and wiped off a rivulet of rainwater running down the side of his face. "I think we'd better get out of these wet clothes."

His eyebrows shot up. "I'm all for that." In spite of his wet clothes and the cold, he heated up again.

"Behave."

"Okay, at least until I get a fire started. I think the temperature is dropping."

"Do we have any dry wood?" she asked.

"Yeah, back here," he said, gesturing to a wood box that had been left full. It was a rule for anyone who used the place.

"Good."

While he built a fire in the old stone fireplace, Jessica began taking the food out of the saddlebags. "Your mom did pack a lot of food."

"Good, 'cause we may be here awhile. Is there anything there we can heat up to drink?" His gaze fell on her breasts, almost visible through the wet blouse, and he had difficulty concentrating.

"There are two bottles of water and four cans of soda," she said, then sneezed.

"I think we'd better do what you suggested earlier," Cal said, grinning, grateful for her sneeze.

"What was that?"

"Get out of our wet clothes."

Since that action would only increase the likelihood of what Jessica had planned to pursue, she reached for the buttons of her blouse, all too eager to comply.

"Wait!" Cal said, jumping to his feet. "First let me find those old blankets we keep here."

Jessica stared at him. After his injury, he hadn't seemed interested in modesty. Was her seduction of Cal Baxter going to be harder than she'd thought?

She watched him as he found the blankets and shook them out. They were old and rough, but she supposed, if one were cold enough, they would be better than nothing.

He handed her one of the blankets. "I'll be a gentleman and turn my back," he said, offering her his place by the fire.

She said nothing, but she took the blanket and moved closer to the fire. Cal turned his back, unbuttoning his shirt as he did so. Jessica made quick work of stripping off her sweater. As she unfastened her jeans, she kept her eyes on Cal, admiring the way his broad back tapered to narrow hips. She wasn't going to pass up the opportunity to admire his physique.

Her jeans sank to the floor as his did, weighted down by the water. But she'd forgotten to remove her boots first, distracted by his unrobing. She hurriedly did so, knowing he was going to turn around quickly.

"Are you ready?" he asked, his back still to her.

"Just a minute," she said as she discarded the jeans. She'd worn matching peach underwear, which she left on. As she picked up the blanket, she said, "Okay," knowing he would catch sight of the peach ensemble. She wanted to whet his appetite.

Cal turned around, expecting to see Jessica wrapped in a blanket. Instead, he caught a delicious sight of peach silk barely covering her golden skin. Then the blanket fell into place and he began breathing again.

"Uh, are you hungry?" he asked, his voice husky.

"Sure. Breakfast was early this morning," she confessed, a pleasant smile on her face, as if it didn't bother her that they were alone and nearly nude.

Obviously she wasn't as affected as he. Now he was really grateful for the blanket since it hid his outrageous response to her body. Without it he'd be embarrassed to face her, much less try to eat.

With his blanket held in place with his left hand, he picked up one of the packs of food she'd taken out of the saddlebag.

Jessica followed him to the table. "Are we going to sit here, or by the fire?"

"Which do you prefer? It's still kind of cold over here," he said, indicating the table.

"By the fire." She picked up a can of soda and put it between her arm and her body so she could pick up a second can. "It's going to take us a while to transfer everything since we can only use one hand." As she moved to the fire, her blanket drooped, exposing a soft shoulder and a peach strap.

Cal's gaze was glued to that shoulder, and he held his breath in case it slipped farther. "Uh, maybe you should just sit down and I'll bring everything over."

"Okay," she agreed, and sank to her knees.

He took his blanket and wrapped it around his waist, tying the corners in a knot. Then he grabbed a bag of chips, as well as the sandwiches, and joined Jessica.

"Aren't you cold without something on your chest?" Jessica asked. Then she frowned and said, "I see your bruise. You're right about the discoloration. Does it hurt all over?"

"Nah. Here, Mom made roast beef sandwiches."

When she reached for the sandwich he offered, her blanket slipped again, revealing a tempting amount of décolletage that left his mouth dry.

"Uh, want some potato chips?" he offered, hoping to distract himself before he completely lost his appetite. He intended to seduce her, but not until after lunch. He felt he should talk to her first, explain why they should share that intimacy.

Convince her with words.

Damn, he hoped he could figure out the right ones.

When the sandwiches had been eaten, or at least part of them, because Jessica didn't appear to be any hungrier than he was, she asked, "What did your mother send for dessert? I hope it's some of her oatmeal cookies. They're my favorite."

"Sounds like a good guess. Mom likes to make you happy."

"Your parents are so wonderful, Cal," Jessica said, a smile on her sexy lips.

He didn't want to talk about his parents. He wasn't sure they'd approve of what he intended. Not that he would force Jess. Of course not. But anticipating their wedding vows, particularly wedding vows that were a fantasy, probably wouldn't have their approval.

He got up and went over to the table for the small box labeled Dessert. A quick look over his shoulder showed Jessica staring at the fire, so he took advantage of her inattention to pull the condoms from his back jeans' pocket.

Then he frowned. How could he hide them in the blanket? Finally, he shoved the package under the edge of the blanket at his back, and returned to the fire.

Once he got down to the floor again, he looked at the box in his hands. Somehow he didn't think he could continue to pretend an interest in cookies. He decided to give her a choice.

"Baby, I have something for you. I mean, I have something to tell you."

"Okay," she said, her gaze wide.

"When I was hurt…" He trailed off, wondering if he was starting the right way.

"I wanted to talk about that, too," she hurriedly said.

"You're not going to try to talk me out of being sheriff again, are you?" he asked, distracted.

"No," she said slowly. "I realize you're right. Sheriff is who you are. And...and I like you the way you are."

Like? That wasn't what he wanted. But he'd known he had some persuading to do.

She continued. "So, what did you have to tell me?"

"You can go first."

"Uh, maybe we should eat the cookies first."

He'd forgotten about the box in his hands. "Okay." He broke the tape with his thumb. "Mom didn't want us to open these by accident, did she? Must be really special cookies."

"Yes." She watched his every move, as if he'd pull a rabbit out of the box.

Lifting the lid, he brushed back some tissue, then stared.

Jessica leaned forward. "What is it?"

He slid the box behind him. "Uh, nothing."

"Nothing?"

"Just a joke. Mom has a weird sense of humor."

She leaned closer. "Let me see."

"No, really, Jess, it's not—"

She grabbed his arm and tugged.

He wasn't about to get into a wrestling match with her, particularly not while she was wrapped in a blanket that had trouble staying put when she wasn't moving.

Surrendering the box, he watched her face. She pulled back the lid and tissue and stared, as he had.

Then she burst out laughing.

"Jess?"

She reached behind her, beneath the edge of the blanket, and pulled out a package of condoms, matching the ones in the box. Her lips trembled as she stared at Cal.

He had no option but to show his own hand. With a grin, he reached behind him and pulled the condoms from his back. "Great minds," he said.

Jessica stared at the condoms in their hands and in the box. Then she dropped hers, took the blanket edges in her hands, and peeled it from her body. "I think it's unanimous."

Chapter Fifteen

Cal's gaze devoured her beautiful body, clad only in a peach-colored bra and bikini panties. His blanket fell to the wayside, also, as he reached out for her.

"Baby, you are so beautiful," he whispered, his hands traveling from her slim shoulders to her full breasts, down to her slender waist and settling on her curvaceous hips. He lifted her toward him, eager to feel her against him, flesh to flesh.

Her arms wrapped around his neck as she allowed him to touch her where he wanted. Her lips covered his with an eagerness that filled him with desire.

It didn't take long before he'd removed the two pieces of clothing she still wore. She encouraged him to rid himself of his briefs, too. Then they lay together beside the fire, body to body, mouth to mouth, soul to soul.

Cal couldn't stop stroking her flesh. She was so soft, so fragile, so delicate. The gardenia scent he always associated with Jessica filled his nostrils, as if he were lying in a bed of flowers. His lips left hers to caress her neck, then her breasts.

"Oh, Cal." She sighed, her luscious body moving under him. "Oh, I need—"

"Tell me what you need, baby. I want to make you happy," he muttered before his lips returned to hers. He wanted to make her so happy she couldn't live without him.

Because he was sure his happiness depended on Jessica.

Jessica had wondered what all the excitement was about sex, after her one experience with it. Now she understood. Understood so much that she could scarcely think. Deep inside, she craved Cal, to consume her, to love her, forever.

When his lips trailed down her body, she reached for him, again, pulling him closer. "Now, Cal. Now."

"Okay, let me protect you, baby," Cal whispered, and reached for the multitude of condoms available. For some reason, he wanted to use the ones he'd brought. It was his responsibility. He wanted to protect Jessica.

He ripped open the packet and prepared himself, then returned to Jessica. He couldn't believe how much she touched him, emotionally even more than physically. His Jessica. It only seemed right that they be one.

When he entered her, he found her tight. Slowly, moving inch by incredible inch, he filled her, using his hands and mouth to distract her from any pain. Slanting his mouth across hers, he used his tongue to recreate the action his body was pursuing. When hers followed his into his mouth, he sucked it deeper.

As her body adjusted to him, he began to move,

and she followed, encouraging him with small sounds that teased him, excited him. When he felt her tense beneath him, reaching her peak, he, too, let go, spiraling out of control.

JESSICA LAY AGAINST CAL, sated, content. She loved him so much. She never wanted to leave his side.

Through the years she'd imagined how it would be, loving Cal, but nothing could compare to the reality of Cal's hard, muscular body against hers, his big arms holding her, making her feel safe and excited at the same time.

His lips, those glorious lips, touching her all over.

She wanted more. Greediness filled her and she reached for him again, her hands tracing his sculptured muscles. Her fingers were drawn to his chest as she covered the bruise he'd sustained in that frightening incident.

Her lips followed her hands and she felt Cal respond to her temptation. Her smile widened. "You're so strong."

"I'm going to be weak afterward but it'll be worth it." He paused, a minute later, to choose another condom, before he recreated the excitement for her again.

Later, as they lay in each other's arms, unable to move, she drifted in her happiness, not thinking at all.

Until Cal asked the one question she didn't want to answer.

"Why?"

Jessica pulled away from his warmth and looked

for one of the blankets to wrap around her. She also kept her face turned from his gaze.

"Why what?"

He sat up, magnificent in his nudity, unconscious of the picture he presented. "Why did you want to make love?"

She stood, tucking the blanket over her breasts. It was ridiculous to be this conscious of her body after she'd allowed him so much freedom with it, but suddenly she felt vulnerable.

He hadn't wanted to marry her. Still didn't. So she couldn't confess her love to him without appearing pitiful in his eyes. Forcing what she hoped was a bright, sophisticated smile on her lips, she said, "I wanted to give you a gift. Because I'm grateful you survived." She risked a quick glance at him then moved over to the table and opened a second can of soda.

"Besides, you're a sexy man, Cal Baxter. I'm only human." *And my heart is breaking.*

He shrugged his shoulders. "You're the one with the beauty, baby. You take my breath away."

But I want your heart! Trying to hide her dismay, she picked up the other soda. "Want a drink?"

"No, thanks."

The silence seemed to stretch on forever. Finally he stood, picking up his briefs as he did. He stepped into them with no self-consciousness, while she watched.

"It's still raining. Maybe we'd better hang our clothes next to the fire so they'll be dry when we head for home," he suggested.

He moved to the table and picked up the two

chairs, putting them in front of the fire, their backs facing it. Then he took her blouse and jeans, hanging them off one chair, and his jeans and shirt on the other.

"You want your undies?" he asked, as if he were offering her a newspaper. Then, holding her panties and bra up, he smiled at her. "They're good-looking. I wouldn't want you to lose them."

She snatched them from his hand. "Of course I want them." He sounded so casual, so matter-of-fact, while she still had trouble breathing. She turned away to the farthest corner of the cabin and tried to put them on while keeping the blanket around her shoulders, her back to Cal.

"It's not like I haven't seen you," he said softly.

She glared at him over her shoulder. "I just... It's different."

"Well, come on back to the fire. Even with the blanket, it's cold in here."

"Maybe you should use the other blanket. I'm perfectly warm." She hoped he took her advice. It was difficult not to stare at his muscular physique. The physique she'd just loved with every inch of her.

"Guess I'd better pick up all these condoms. We might have need of them...sometime," he said, his gaze landing on Jessica before turning away.

Did that mean he intended to make love to her again? Now that they'd passed that boundary, did he think it was a given that as long as they were engaged, they would share their bodies?

Could she stand it, knowing that it was a passing thing with him? That he didn't want her, just her body? Her teeth sank into her bottom lip.

"Damn!" he suddenly roared. He was staring at the condoms in his hands.

"What's wrong?"

"Uh, nothing," he said, putting his hands behind his back and staring at her.

"What? What upset you?"

"I'm not upset. I wonder how long it will rain," he said, and walked to the window.

She watched him go. Then she looked back at the floor. The two packages of condoms they'd bought were there, but the box from Mabel was on its side, empty. "Where are the condoms from Mabel?"

"Here. I'll put them in the box. We'll tell her we didn't want dessert. It will drive her crazy."

"May I see them first?" she asked, walking over to him.

"Why? They're just like the others. There's no—"

She snatched one from his hand. He seemed to have spoken the truth. She slowly turned the foil packet in the firelight. Then stopped.

It had tiny little holes in it that only showed when the light hit the foil at a certain angle. Jessica supposed the holes were made by a needle being driven through the packet again and again.

"She didn't!"

Cal hung his head. "She did. I'm ashamed of her, Jess, and I promise I'll talk to her."

"Do they all have holes?" she asked, wondering if they were to have played Russian roulette.

"All of them. She wants a grandchild big-time."

"Did we use any of hers?" Her heart was beating faster at the thought of carrying Cal's child.

"No. I took both of the ones we used from the package I bought. We're safe."

His relief, obvious on his face, depressed her even more. Of course he didn't want her pregnant. He didn't want to marry her. And she knew he would if she became pregnant. Cal was a stand-up kind of guy.

Cal stared at Jessica, disturbed by her unhappiness. He was glad she wasn't pregnant because he didn't want her to feel trapped. He wanted her, with all his heart. But only if she wanted to be with him.

His mother had screwed up. And he was going to let her know about it as soon as they got back. He looked for something to distract Jessica. "Hey, I think I'll finish my sandwich now. Suddenly I'm hungry. How about you?"

She shrugged her shoulders and turned back to the window. "How much longer do you think the rain will last?"

"I don't know. I'll call Dad and let him know we're safe and we'll spend the night here. With all this rain, we won't be able to get back over the creek for ten or twelve hours. It's not the Hilton, but the cabin will keep us safe."

He'd put his phone in the saddlebag, which had kept it dry. He made the connection, but there was a lot of static. "Dad?"

"Yeah. That you, boy?"

"Yeah. We're in the cabin. We're staying the night."

"You okay?"

"Yeah, fine. See you tomorrow."

He put the phone back in the saddlebag. "Well, at least they won't worry about us."

But he was worried. Jessica was acting uneasy, uncomfortable. He tried to think of something to make her relax.

"Don't you want to eat? Mom packed another sandwich for each of us. There's not a lot of variety, but it's filling."

"Maybe later." She didn't turn around.

"Baby, did I hurt you? You know I wouldn't hurt you for anything in the world." He came up behind her and wrapped his arms around her, blanket and all.

She shook her head. "No, of course not."

"Then why won't you look at me?"

She turned in his arms, her gaze meeting his. "You're being ridiculous. I think I'll take that sandwich, after all. I spent all my energy somewhere else." With a bright smile, she pulled from his arms and walked to the table.

He followed her, and they both took their food to the fireplace. Jessica sat and leaned back against the chair holding her clothes.

"The fire feels good."

"Yeah." Great. Dynamite conversation.

"Will your dad call your office to let them know you're stuck out here?"

"Probably not. We'll be back at the ranch early in the morning. There's no reason for anyone to know." He stared at her. "Why?"

"I just thought…it would probably be best if no one knows we…were here."

"Are you ashamed about what happened here?"

"No! But I'm not interested in sharing my private life with the rest of Cactus."

He was. He wanted everyone to know Jessica was his lady. But he could wait. He would wait. It had to be her choice.

THE RAIN STOPPED about dusk. Cal removed the bridles from the horses and turned them out into the old corral. There was enough grass growing there to feed them.

Jessica, left inside alone, discovered their clothes were dry. She dressed, feeling more confident in her clothes. Then she tidied the cabin.

When she gathered the two saddlebags together to place in a nearby corner, she discovered another package Cal hadn't unpacked. Oatmeal-raisin cookies.

Jessica put them on the table. They would make a good breakfast in the morning. Or the best they could manage until they got back to the ranch.

In the one cupboard, she found a kerosene lamp. She put it on the table to wait for Cal's return. He could handle that better than her. But at least the lamp would allow them more light than the fireplace gave off.

She returned to the cupboard and discovered something that brought a grin to her lips. An old deck of cards. Cal had taught her how to play poker when she was eight.

Testing her skills against Cal's, like old times, would be a lot better than sitting around in the dark, wondering if he intended to make love to her again.

The cabin door opened and her moments of peace were gone. Cal had returned.

"Look what I found," she said, smiling.

He seemed to respond to her relaxed air. "The lamp? You're excited about that?"

She pulled the deck of cards from behind her back. "Nope. I'm excited about this. Want to challenge me to a game of poker? We've got matches."

"Matches, huh? What are they worth?"

She paused to consider. "I don't want to ruin you, so how about a penny a piece?"

"You sure you can afford to lose that much?" he teased as he worked on lighting the lamp, using one of those matches. As it lit, he adjusted the flame, then set it in the center of the table. "Hey, you've got your clothes on," he suddenly said.

"As perceptive as you are, it'll be a wonder if I win any matches," she said in mock wonder.

"Watch it, woman," he growled in return. "I went out in my blanket to take care of your horse. Why didn't you say the clothes were dry?"

Her smile relaxed. "I didn't think to check. Ready to play?"

"Let me put on my clothes. Then I'll be red-hot."

He already was red-hot as far as Jessica was concerned. And when he touched her, he set her on fire.

Several hours later it appeared that Jessica had all the luck.

"I'd accuse you of cheating if I hadn't dealt that hand," Cal finally said.

"It must just be my luck. Good thing we're not playing strip poker, or you would've been naked a long time ago," she returned, then caught her breath at the picture in her head. She only hoped the old saying, "lucky in cards, unlucky in love" wasn't true, or he'd never make love to her again. The tension that filled her made the past hour's pastime a waste. She knew what she wanted. She'd give all her matches for Cal's heart.

"I might've played harder if it would've meant you without your clothes. That's called incentive," he said with a grin. Then he added, "Let's call it a night. We need to be up at first light so I won't be late to the office."

He was thinking about tomorrow. She was worried about tonight.

"Um, okay. I need to make a trip outdoors."

"You want to take the lamp?"

"No, the moon's out."

When she returned a few minutes later, Cal had done the housekeeping. One blanket covered the old mattress lying on a platform in the corner. The other was folded on one of the chairs.

"My turn," Cal said, and stepped outside.

She stared at the small bed in the corner. Did he intend to sleep on the floor? And where did she want him to sleep?

That was the hardest question. She wanted to love Cal again, but she didn't know if she should. She'd already realized how hard loving him would be when he didn't feel the same way.

With a sigh, she looked at the bed again. Tonight, maybe she'd let him make the choice. One more time in his arms, one long night next to him, might be all she'd ever have. She shivered at the thought of his touch. Could she live without Cal in her bed?

Cal returned.

"You're not going to sleep in your jeans, are you?" he asked, a smile on his face.

She didn't smile. "Are you going to sleep on the floor?" Her heartbeat stopped as she waited for his answer.

His head snapped up and he stared at her. "Do you want me to?"

God help her, all she could do was shake her head no.

"Good," he said with a gentle smile. Then he picked up the second blanket and nodded toward the bed. "We'll need each other's body heat to stay warm."

Just thinking about sharing that small space with Cal was already warming Jessica.

"Slip off your clothes and get under the cover, sweetheart. I'll turn out the lamp and join you as soon as I put more wood on the fire."

With her back to him, she slid out of her sweater and jeans. Should she leave on her underwear? No, she was too honest for that. She wanted him to make love to her.

Removing her bra and panties, she put them on top of her clothes and slid under the cover.

He built up the blaze with several more logs, then removed his own clothes. She watched wide-eyed, enjoying the sight of his hard body. The fact that he was already aroused before he'd even joined her in the small bed filled her with joy and started a blaze in her heart and body that lasted long into the night.

THERE WASN'T MUCH conversation the next morning. Jessica brought out the oatmeal cookies and they opened the last soda. The sun was rising in the east as they went to the corral to saddle the horses.

"Can you manage?" she asked Cal, remembering he'd said lifting hurt.

"Yeah. Are you warm enough?"

The air was brisk this morning, as it sometimes could be in late October, but her sweater was warm. "I'm fine."

"I could get you one of the blankets."

"No. You're the one who's only wearing a shirt." Such dull conversation, after an incredible night. Even this morning, when awkwardness filled the air again, she'd delighted in waking up in Cal's arms.

They managed the ride home with little trouble and even less talk. As soon as they'd taken care of the animals, Cal offered her the use of his second shower while he used the master bath.

"I'll wait until I get home," she assured him. "Can you drop me off on your way to the office?"

"Of course. I'll hurry."

She spent the ten minutes he was upstairs in the kitchen, cooking eggs and bacon. Even more importantly, she made a pot of coffee. Half a soda didn't provide enough caffeine.

"I smell coffee," Cal called as he rumbled down the stairs.

Jessica almost burst into tears. How normal he sounded. How wonderful. How impossible. She turned her back and poured him a mug of coffee.

"How about some food, too?" she offered.

"I wouldn't turn that down," he assured her with

a smile. "Especially from the second-best cook in the county."

"Second-best?" Jessica challenged, her brows rising, grateful for his teasing to erase her sentimentality.

He took the cup from her and dropped a casual kiss on her lips. "If Mom heard I thought she wasn't the best cook in the county, you know she'd never feed me again. You don't mind being second-best, do you?"

"Of course not," she told him with a smile before adding, "as long as you don't expect *me* to cook for you!" Since she set a full plate in front of him, she knew he wouldn't take her seriously.

"Hmm, I know. You can be first in something else, something that won't put you in competition with Mom."

"What?"

Having sat at the table with his plate of food, he grabbed her around the waist and pulled her onto his lap. "You can be number one in my bed, baby." Then he kissed her.

She pushed her way up out of his lap. "Eat your breakfast."

He frowned. "We haven't talked about last night," he said, watching her.

What was there to talk about? They'd had good sex. Great sex. And she'd loved him, as she had for years. But, for him, apparently, that's all it was.

"Um, there's no time this morning."

"Jess, I want you to know I've never experienced anything like that, anything that incredible, before."

Great. He thought she was really good at sex.

She said nothing and he chewed the bite he'd just placed in his mouth forever.

Finally he said, "Aren't you going to say anything?"

Stiffening, she raised her gaze to his silver eyes. "You mean you want me to say it was good for me, too? I thought you already knew that."

"A man likes to know," he assured her, a lopsided grin on his beloved face.

"Well, your reputation is intact as a lady-killer, Cal Baxter. No fear."

"That's not what—"

"Time to go or you're going to be late," she said, jumping up from the table and putting her dishes in the sink. Then she hurried for his truck, determined to end the conversation before she started crying.

CAL DROPPED JESSICA OFF at her town house and headed for the office, after a searing goodbye kiss.

But he was uneasy.

Sex with Jessica had been more than he'd ever imagined it could be. Never had he physically been so satisfied. Satisfied, hell. He hadn't been sure he'd ever stand upright again.

But he needed more than that. He needed to know that Jessica wanted to be with him for everything life had to offer. Not just the physical pleasure. To share the joy, the pain—to have those four kids he suddenly wanted.

But their conversation at the breakfast table hadn't been reassuring. He'd had to press her just to get a response on their lovemaking, much less the future.

But he wasn't going to give up. Or stop loving her.

"Hey, Cal, how was your day off?" Pete asked, a smirk on his face.

"Great, Pete. You get in any trouble while I was gone?"

"Nope. Nothing, I promise."

"Good." He passed through the big office into his own. As soon as he sat, he picked up the phone and dialed Jess's number.

When she answered, he said, "Hey, baby, I forgot to mention something."

"What?"

"I think you should move your things out to the ranch. Then we could take early morning rides and see a lot more of each other." Especially at night.

Silence.

He began to sweat. Was she already through with him?

"I'm not sure that's a good idea, Cal. I have a lot of work to do for the restaurant. I'll need to be here."

"Ah. I'd forgotten about the restaurant."

"I'm meeting Jeff at the site again today. I want to go over everything one more time before I sign the contract."

"Baby, I'm not sure opening another restaurant would be a good idea. I mean, it will take so much of your time." Time away from him. He was greedy; he wanted her with him every minute.

More silence.

Then she spoke quietly, almost sadly. "But, Cal, if I don't have my restaurant, what will I do with myself? I can't just sit around all day."

"But—"

"I have to go. I'm meeting Jeff in fifteen minutes."

He hung up the phone. They were going to have to talk, he and Jess. But not over the phone. The best time would be after they'd made love, when they lay in each other's arms. Then he could tell her that he never wanted to let her go.

That he loved her.

The door to his office opened and Betty's head appeared. "Cal? I knocked, but you didn't answer. Are you all right? You look hot."

Oh, yeah.

Chapter Sixteen

Jessica spent most of the day at the location she'd selected. She and Jeff went over it inch by inch, calculating costs and discussing options.

She couldn't figure out what was wrong. Everything seemed to be fine, but her heart wasn't in it. When she'd started The Old Cantina, she'd worked night and day, driven by the excitement.

Today, her thoughts, her hopes, her dreams were centered on Cal, not The Last Roundup.

"I don't know, Jeff. Something doesn't feel right," she finally said.

He frowned and checked the pages on his clipboard. "Everything looks okay to me, Jess, but it's your decision, of course."

She rubbed her forehead. "Maybe it's just a bad day. Let's stop now. I'll take the figures home and study them, then call you in the morning."

"Okay. I'll go over everything again, too. Maybe I missed something."

She smiled wearily and led the way back out to their two vehicles, shaking hands and sending him back to Lubbock.

Leaving her to deal with the real problem. Her future. She knew what she wanted, but it was out of her hands. Cal was the key to her happiness.

But if she couldn't have Cal, she'd need something to keep her busy.

Cal's baby would give her a reason to go on.

She scrubbed that thought at once. She had promised herself she wasn't going to trap him. But she wished she had an answer to her problem.

What was she going to do?

"ARE WE PLAYING TONIGHT?" Edith Hauk asked Mabel over the telephone.

"As far as I know. It's my turn to be hostess. I'll call the others." Mabel called her other two friends as soon as Edith hung up. "Bridge tonight?"

The other two agreed, and Mabel hung up the phone. It was hard to concentrate on bridge when she was waiting to hear from Cal or Jessica.

She'd done a terrible thing. She knew it. But the result would be wonderful. Mabel knew if Jessica turned up pregnant, the children would marry at once.

That was what she wanted.

But she felt bad about tricking them. And Ed would kill her if he ever found out.

But she hadn't done it to win the bet. Oh, sure, that would be fun, but the most important part was that Jessica and Cal find each other. Something about the engagement didn't seem quite legitimate. She was only trying to make sure they would carry through.

"Mabel? You heard from Cal or Jessica?" Ed asked from the kitchen.

"Um, no, I haven't."

"Why don't you call Jess? Just to be sure they got back."

"I already did. She didn't answer. Do you want me to call Cal at the office?" She didn't really want to call Cal, but it would be good to know they got back all right. And besides, she didn't think he would've noticed what she'd done to the condoms. He'd be irritated with her because she'd included them, of course. Unless he hadn't thought to bring any.

Ed agreed she should call Cal.

When he answered the phone, she spoke quickly, hoping he wouldn't notice her nervousness. "Hi, dear. Your father wanted to be sure the two of you got back all right."

"We're back. And, Mom, you and I have to have a talk."

"Oh. I was only suggesting—"

"You were trying to get Jessica pregnant."

She sucked in a deep breath. Ed was watching her from the kitchen door. "They're back, Ed. Everything's fine."

Thankfully, Ed nodded his head and disappeared.

"I—I—you said you wanted children."

"If you do anything else as underhanded as you did with the condoms, you won't be allowed to hold the first child for a year."

She gasped. "Cal! You can't mean it!"

"I mean it. Don't force Jessica into anything. Okay?"

Sniffing, she nodded. Then, realizing he couldn't see her, she said, "I promise."

As he was about to hang up, she remembered to ask one more question. "Does…does Jessica know what I—"

"Yes. I'm not sure she'll forgive you."

And he hung up the phone.

CAL WAS FRUSTRATED. He'd been trying to reach Jessica most of the afternoon. He thought about going to the building she was going to buy, the one she and Jeff had looked at across the square from the sheriff's office.

Every time he'd called her town house and gotten no answer, he'd walked to the front of the office and look to see if her Lexus was still parked in front of the building.

"It's still there," Betty finally said after the fourth time. "Why don't you walk over and see how she's doing?"

"I'm too busy," he growled, and stomped back into his office.

Suddenly the radio emitted static, then an excited voice. "Woowee! We got a movie star or something heading our way. A big black limo is about three miles out of town."

Cal stepped around Betty's desk and picked up the microphone. "Calm down, Ricky. Anyone can hire a limo. How do you know it's coming here?"

"Well, it has to, boss."

"But it probably won't stop. Just do your job, okay?"

"Yeah, boss," a subdued Ricky replied.

Betty glared at him. "You may be in a bad mood, but there's no need to make Ricky have a bad day."

Because he felt guilty for exactly that, he ignored Betty and retreated to his office.

A limo? Must be some big-city guy.

Could it be another man Jessica had never told him about? The last time it had been Jeff, a married man. He'd almost forgotten his idea that she loved a specific man. Could she have made love to him while she loved someone else? That thought disturbed him.

He didn't want to believe she cared about someone else. But she hadn't told him she didn't. He worried over the whole situation again. Was there really someone?

He'd thought maybe she'd made the man up because there didn't seem to be anyone she was interested in from Cactus. Did this limo explain that little problem? Was she in love with someone she'd met from a big city?

Was he going to lose her?

He leaped to his feet and rushed out of his office, heading for the square.

"She's gone," Betty announced as he reached the front door.

"How long ago?"

"About two minutes."

He stood there, undecided, staring out at the square. When he saw a black limo pull to a halt at the one stoplight, he opened the door and stepped outside.

The light turned green and the limo moved forward slowly. He tried to see inside, but the windows were darkly tinted. Then it stopped alongside him, and the front window went down.

"Excuse me, Officer, but where would we find The Old Cantina?"

JESSICA SAT at her kitchen table.

She was too weary to climb the stairs, too worried to cook any food, too discouraged to make any decisions.

The phone rang.

"Jess, it's Nita. Some high-muck-a-mucks from the company that bought you out are here. They wanted me to call, to see if you could meet them for dinner at seven."

Jessica frowned, trying to work out the significance of the men's arrival. She had visited with them a number of times during the negotiations. "Yes, of course I can. Did they say why they're here?"

"No. That's all they said, just could you come eat with them. But they seem happy."

"Okay, thanks, Nita. I'll be there."

She hung up the phone, concentrating on the conversation, her hand resting on the receiver, when it rang again.

She picked it up at once.

"Hi, baby. How'd your day go?" It was Cal.

She shivered, stirred just by hearing his voice. "Fine."

"Will you let me take you to dinner?"

"I can't."

Before she could explain about what had happened, he said, "Jess, you can't shut me out."

"I'm not trying to, Cal. Some of the officers of

the TGM Corporation are in town, at The Old Cantina. They want me to have dinner with them.''

"Why?"

"I don't know. But I promised I'd be there at seven.''

"Would you let me come with you? I promise I won't interfere, but I don't like you facing these guys alone.''

Cal to the rescue. But she wouldn't mind a little support tonight. "Okay.''

He didn't respond, and she wondered if he'd changed his mind. "Cal? Do you want to come?"

"Yeah. What time do I pick you up?"

"We're supposed to be there by seven.''

"Right, I'll pick you up at six forty-five.''

CAL WENT HOME and showered and shaved again. Then he took one of his business suits, seldom worn in Cactus, out of the closet. But he knew big-city executives wouldn't be dressed in jeans. And he didn't want Jess ashamed of him.

Besides, he had plans for after dinner that didn't include anyone from Dallas. Tonight, he was going to be honest with Jessica, tell her he loved her. Ask her to marry him. And hope and pray she'd give him a chance.

It occurred to him that he should've proposed at the line cabin last night. Then he'd have the right to demand she refuse any offer these men made. And they had come to make an offer, he was sure.

But he couldn't, wouldn't, keep Jessica from doing what would make her happy. He just hoped he was what she wanted.

He pulled up in her driveway at the exact time he'd promised. When she opened the door to his knock, he sucked in his breath. She was wearing a tailored forest-green suit, with a silk vee-neck blouse. Gold earrings were her only jewelry except for her emerald and diamond ring.

The sight of his ring on her finger filled him with pride. She was going to meet these men with his brand on her. He liked that.

He helped her into his truck, then joined her. "Have you figured out what's going on?"

"No, unless they've heard about my new restaurant."

"Think they'll give you some grief over it?"

"No. I called Alex again, just to be sure, but she told me they have no ground to stand on."

"Then we'll relax and enjoy our meal—on them."

They didn't talk much on the short drive to the restaurant, but Cal was encouraged when he took her hand in his before they walked into the restaurant and she didn't pull away.

They approached the table around which sat three men in suits. Everyone else in the restaurant was dressed in jeans and boots.

Cal was proud of Jessica as she calmly greeted the three men who stood. "Gentlemen, welcome back to Cactus. I hope you don't mind that my fiancé, Cal Baxter, accompanied me."

Yep, he was proud of her.

"Not at all. Welcome, Mr. Baxter," the first man said. The other two nodded, and one of them reached for another chair.

As soon as they were seated, Nita appeared. "Jess, what would you and Cal like to drink?"

"Iced tea," she replied, and Cal nodded.

"I'll have those nachos right out, sir," Nita said to one of the gentleman and quickly disappeared. No chitchatting as usual.

Jessica, however, had social chitchat down to an art. Cal listened in amazement as she carried the conversation, discussing weather and travel until both their iced teas and the nachos had been delivered to their table.

During the nachos, the conversation turned to their engagement and questions about Cal's occupation. He answered calmly, but he was thinking about better ways of spending his evening...with Jess.

When the meals they'd ordered had been delivered and the men seemed to be settling in to an evening with no significant information to be discussed, Jessica cut to the chase.

"Okay, I know you didn't travel all the way out here to eat at one of your new restaurants. Why are you here?"

All three men put down their silverware and looked at her. Finally, the one next to Jessica—Bill, he thought—nodded.

"You're right, Jessica. Our manager here reported that you were thinking of opening another restaurant."

"Yes."

"Our contract says—"

"It's not a Mexican restaurant, Bill. It's a steak house. I checked with my attorney, and our contract doesn't restrict me in that area."

"We know, but—well, we have a proposition for you."

JESSICA HAD A LOT to think about. And some of it didn't even have anything to do with Cal.

The corporation had an offer for her, but they didn't want to discuss details until after they tasted her new steak recipe tomorrow. She hadn't really wanted to cook for them, but she'd felt she owed them consideration.

"Will you come to lunch tomorrow?" she asked Cal.

He hadn't spoken since they'd left the restaurant.

"Of course I will, if you want me."

"I do," she said, her voice husky as she thought how true those words were. Sitting circumspectly on her side of the front seat, she longed for him to slide across and reach for her, to pull her into a kiss like the one they'd shared last night.

Instead, he merely asked, "What do you think they're going to offer you?"

"I don't know."

"Will it mean moving to Dallas?"

She stared at him. Was he hoping to get rid of her? Did he actually want her to leave Cactus?

She was within a breath of asking him, of laying it all out on the line. Telling him how she felt about him, how she'd always felt about him. But when she opened her mouth, no words came out. Only a sigh.

"Well, you must have lots to do to get ready for tomorrow, so I won't come in," Cal said. He wasn't even looking at her now. "In case I forget to tell you tomorrow, good luck."

Jessica felt as if a pail of ice water had suddenly been dumped on her head. How could this be the same man as the one who shared the line shack with her last night? The one who brought her body to a fever pitch with one touch? No, this man was too cold and unemotional. Next thing she knew he'd reach out and shake her hand.

Without even so much as a glance in his direction, she opened the truck door and ran for home.

IT TOOK EVERY OUNCE of willpower he possessed to let her go. He didn't want to. He'd hoped to explain himself this evening. To tell her he wanted their engagement to be real. To spend this night—and every night of the rest of his life—with Jessica in his arms.

But he didn't want to discuss what could determine the rest of their lives while she was distracted by business. And he could tell she was distracted.

He didn't sleep well that night. Without Jessica beside him, curled around him as she'd been last night, he couldn't settle down. He tossed and turned, and woke up feeling more exhausted than when he went to bed.

After he reached the office, he dialed Jess's number.

"Hi, baby," he said softly when she answered. "Are you doing all right?"

She sounded tired, too. "Of course. I'm fine."

"Anything I can do to help with today's luncheon?"

"No. Just be here for me."

"Always. I missed you last night."

There was silence on her end.

He'd intended to wait until after the luncheon, until after she'd spoken with the corporate execs. He wanted Jessica to be free to make her own decisions about her future. But he was frightened. What if she didn't love him and want to be with him? He couldn't face the rest of his life without Jessica.

"Jess, I have to—"

"There's the timer on the stove. I'll see you at noon," she said quickly before hanging up the phone.

Cal sat there, the receiver in his hand. Had he waited too long? Had he already lost her?

JESSICA FOUGHT her nerves all morning.

She hadn't slept well. But the worry over her and Cal's relationship had eased any nerves she had over the luncheon.

She'd decided the smart business decision was to listen to whatever offers the corporation made. Right now she had no idea where she stood with Cal, whether she had a future with him and in Cactus. She owed it to herself to hear the execs out.

Suddenly she wanted to wow them with her new idea. It all came down to personal pride. She went into the dining room to recheck every detail.

Ambience was important. She'd used a pale yellow tablecloth with green place mats. In the center of the table were several small cactus plants and a grouping of yellow squash.

When the doorbell rang, she hurried to the door, hoping it was Cal. Instead, her three visitors strolled in. She settled them into her living room and served fried zucchini with drinks while they waited for Cal.

After what seemed like hours of small talk she checked her watch. Cal was twenty minutes late. Did he intend to show up at all? In spite of how they'd parted last night, that wasn't like Cal. She excused herself and called his office, her heart thumping as she considered his response.

Betty answered the phone.

"Betty, it's Jess. Where's Cal?"

"Oh, hon, I'm sorry. He's settling an argument between Herk Jones and his neighbor. Is anything wrong?"

"He was supposed to be here for lunch at noon. I…just got worried."

"Oh, my gosh. I bet he's forgotten the time. Those two have been going at each other for an hour. I'll go tell him. I'll be right back."

"Thanks, Betty."

Betty returned to the phone. "Jess, he said he doesn't know when he'll be there—to go on without him."

After hanging up the phone, she covered her disappointment and invited her guests to the table. After all, she still had a business to manage.

Once the food was served, the three executives dispensed with the chitchat and concentrated on the meal. They asked her several questions about her choices and praised the steaks.

Finally, Bill put down his silverware. "Jessica, I won't beat around the bush. The corporation thinks you're a genius. We'd like to purchase the entire package—your restaurant concept, your new recipe, everything."

Jessica remained silent. She simply stared at him.

Bill cleared his throat. "We haven't mentioned price. That might help convince you."

Jessica straightened her spine and looked Bill in the eye. Two million dollars for a recipe and an unproved restaurant idea. Why was she hesitating?

Apparently the executive misinterpreted her silence. With a quick glance at his cohorts, he came back with a counteroffer. "All right, Ms. Hoya, we'll double the offer. But I'm afraid that's as high as I can go. Of course, it comes with stock options, a corner office, staff. You know. TGM gets the pick of the Dallas elite."

"Dallas?" Did he mean she'd have to leave Cactus? Her home, her friends...Cal? No matter what her dream—no matter how hard she'd worked all her life to rise above her past—was it worth walking away from the man she loved?

But does he love you? an inner voice asked. That was the question.

The offer was tempting, almost too good to refuse. "Well, Bill," she said. "Let's talk further."

"JESSICA'S GOING TO BE real disappointed," Betty pointed out after Cal finally pacified the two men.

"Damn. How did she take it?"

"You know Jessica. She's a strong woman. I sure am going to hate to see her leave Cactus," Betty said as she continued with her filing.

Cal froze. Then he snapped, "What did you say?"

"I said I'm sure—"

"Who said she's leaving?"

Betty looked up at him. "You know I can't reveal my sources."

"Oh, yes, you can." Cal's tone was gruff. He was too impatient to deal with her teasing.

"Nita overheard those men talking. She passed the word along."

Cal closed his eyes, regret filling him. Then he stiffened his shoulders. He wasn't going to give up on Jessica. Or himself.

"Betty, prepare my letter of resignation," he ordered in a no-nonsense voice, and whirled to go back to his office.

"What? What are you talking about, Cal Baxter? You can't resign," Betty yelled. She jumped up from her desk and trod after him, protests continuing to roll from her mouth.

He grabbed his Stetson and his Jeep keys and turned to face her. "Yes, I can. For Jessica, I can do anything. Have that letter ready when I get back." Then he left her standing there with her mouth open.

He was grateful he was the sheriff when he drove way over the speed limit to reach Jessica's town house. At least he didn't have to worry about getting a speeding ticket. All he had to worry about was whether Jessica would let him go with her.

Whether she'd let him be a part of her life.

After pounding on the door, he waited impatiently, his breathing speeding up when he heard her footsteps through the door. As soon as she opened it, he blurted, "Did you accept their offer?"

"Hello to you, too. Don't you want to come in?"

He moved past her. "Yeah. Did you accept their offer?"

"Yes, I did."

He took a deep breath. "I'm turning in my resignation. I'll be ready to go when you are."

"Ready to go where?"

"To Dallas." He reached out and captured her shoulders. "Baby, I can't let you go. I know we said our engagement was a pretense, but—"

"Cal, I don't know what you're talking about. I'm not going to Dallas." She watched him, her green gaze steady, patient.

"You're not going to Dallas?" he asked, incredulous.

"Of course not. Cactus is my home. You're here."

Cal felt relief flow through him. Then, the significance of her words set him on fire. "You want to be with me?"

"Your mother's right," Jessica said with a shaky laugh. "Men are dumb as—"

Cal cut her off when he pulled her close and took possession of her mouth with his. He kissed her with the force of all his feelings, all the words that he'd been afraid to own up to. He let his lips tell her now.

Even as he broke the kiss, he said in an astonished tone, "But you kept talking about marrying someone else! You even let me make up that stupid list."

"You broke my heart with that list." There were tears in her eyes now as she pulled back to look at him.

"I was praying you'd throw it in my face. Instead, you said 'go ahead.' No wonder I was confused." With his thumbs he wiped away the tears and then he kissed her, a long kiss that distracted him from their explanations.

"I was talking about marrying you," she assured

him, her voice breathless. "It's always been about you."

"Why didn't you tell me?"

"I did! What do you think kissing you every time I could, sleeping with you, meant?"

Cal stared at her. "I—I thought maybe you were inexperienced, trying your wings. Or maybe I took advantage of you." He paused, then grinned. "I was so overwhelmed with wanting you, I guess I didn't think clearly."

"I guess not," she drawled.

"Wait a minute. If I was supposed to know kissing me meant you loved me, why didn't you know? Two of us were doing that kissing."

Jessica rolled her eyes. "Really, Cal, that's obvious."

"What is?"

"Men want sex whether they're in love or not. Right?"

"That sounds sexist," he protested, then relented, "But I'm afraid you're right. But it was more than that for me." His lips took hers in a kiss that promised many hot nights...and days, too, for the rest of their life.

When they came up for air, with a lot of heavy breathing, she said, "Have you turned in your resignation yet?"

"Nope. I told Betty to write the letter."

"Which means she's told half the town by now," Jessica whispered as she dropped kisses on Cal's face.

"Mmm," he muttered in agreement, catching her lips with his.

In the midst of that kiss, he realized he hadn't asked some important questions. "You are going to marry me, aren't you?"

"Oh, yes."

Another kiss.

"But you said you took their offer."

"A modified version. I get to stay here in Cactus, have my restaurant, but work for them for a lot of money." She grinned. "I'm quite a negotiator, aren't I?"

"The best. How did you do that?"

"They're going to franchise The Last Roundup, but my franchise is free. And when I come up with other ideas for restaurants, they'll pay me."

A pounding on her door interrupted their embrace.

"Who could that be?"

"Maybe those negotiators are back?"

"No. They're halfway to Dallas," Jessica assured him. Swinging open the door, she discovered the mayor and several city councilmen on her porch. They ignored her and spoke to Cal.

"Cal, you can't quit! We need you. Tell us what you need to make you stay."

Cal grinned and looked at Jessica. "Well, you might be able to persuade me. But it will take some new patrol cars and another deputy."

"Done!" the mayor promised. "Anything else?"

"I think a month's vacation for a honeymoon ought to do it."

When they were finally left to themselves again, Jessica melted into Cal's arms and said, "I guess I'm not the only negotiator in this family."

"Hey, all those things will be good for the county.

Except the month-long honeymoon. That will be good for me.''

''And me.''

''Good. Go pack your bags.''

''I think you're forgetting something.''

He pretended to look puzzled. ''What?''

''The wedding?''

''Nope. I haven't forgotten. I figure three days is long enough, 'cause I don't want to wait any more.''

''Three days?'' she gasped. Then she took his hand and started toward the stairs. ''Okay. And maybe we can negotiate a way to make the waiting easier.''

''Oh, yeah,'' he agreed, eagerly following her.

Epilogue

They actually took a week to prepare for their wedding. Mabel, along with her cohorts, drove the entire town crazy with their plans.

Instead of a bachelor party, Cal had a quiet dinner with his three friends. They all seemed happy for him, but he knew his marriage would change things.

"Guys, we'll always be friends," he said, raising his beer for a toast. "To friends."

"Of course we will," Mac agreed.

"But it's not going to be the same," Spence said slowly. "Not that I would have it any other way. You and Jess are perfect for each other."

"And don't worry," Tuck said. "The three of us will continue to hold out against marriage. *We* won't weaken."

Cal grinned. "If this is weak, I pray I'm weak for the rest of my life."

He thought of those words now as his friends stood beside him at the altar, waiting for Jessica. Even though he knew they wouldn't appreciate his hopes, he wanted for them the same kind of happiness he'd found with Jessica.

When Jessica came down the aisle, she took his breath away. She wore a beautiful silk bridal gown and a fingertip veil that reached her waist, covering her long black hair. But her glowing smile meant more to Cal than anything she wore.

He felt his life had come full circle.

After the ceremony they shared their happiness with their friends at a reception with all the trappings. The baker in town had dropped everything to prepare their huge cake. The florist had called surrounding shops for help, and the church and the reception hall were filled with white gardenias, Cal's special request.

He wrapped his arm around her as they shook hands with their guests. Leaning over, he whispered, "I love you, Mrs. Baxter."

Before she could reply, Mabel and Ed came up to them. "We're so happy," Mabel said, her eyes full of happy tears. "We're all a family. Your mother would be so proud, Jess."

"Thank you, Mabel. I couldn't ask for a better family."

"Aw, you've always been family, little one," Ed said, hugging her. "But now you're going to be the mother of my grandchildren."

Jessica smiled, expecting Mabel to say something, too. But, after a quick look at Cal, she led Ed away.

"What did you say to your mother?"

Cal repeated his threat.

"Cal, you didn't!"

"Hey, she deserved it."

"No, she didn't, and you need to tell her she's forgiven. I don't want any problems in our family."

"Baby, our family has been perfect ever since you showed up. You were the most adorable four-year-old I've ever seen." He pulled her against him again.

"Maybe, in a few years, you'll discover another four-year-old that's even cuter, with silver-gray eyes."

"Or big green ones."

"And if you do, you'll have to stop calling me baby," she noted, laughter and sadness mixed in her voice.

He dropped a warm kiss on her lips. "No one will ever take your place, Jess. You and I belong together."

"I wish Mac, Spence, and Tuck would find someone and be happy, too," she said, catching sight of Mac leaning against the wall.

"Hey, their mothers are as intent on matchmaking as Mom. Concentrate on me, sweetheart. I want all your attention."

With a smile, she whispered, "You've always had my attention, Cal. Long before you ever knew it."

He wrapped his arms around her. "I may be slow to figure some things out, Jess, but once I do, I stick to the course. You're never going to be rid of me."

As her lips joined his, Jessica couldn't think of a better promise.

"WE'RE ALL REALLY HAPPY for you, Mabel, and for those two. They're perfect together," Ruth said, smiling.

Mabel nodded, beaming.

But Ruth wasn't finished. "But don't think you've won our bet!"

"Yeah," Edith said. "Our bet wasn't about getting them married. It was about a grandbaby."

"That's right," Florence agreed. "I certainly haven't given up."

Mabel considered her friends. Then she smiled. After all, she could afford to be charitable. "You're right. And you still have a chance, of course. But I can't help but feel I have a head start."

"So did the hare," Florence pointed out, "but it's the tortoise who won the race."

Mabel sniffed. "At least my hare made it to the church. I'll trust nature to do the rest."

Florence looked at Ruth and Edith and broke out in a smile. "Well, then, we'll just have to give nature a little helping hand for those other three."

HARLEQUIN®
SUPERROMANCE

Due to popular reader demand, Harlequin Superromance® is expanding from 4 to 6 titles per month!

Starting May 1999, you can have more of the kind of stories that you love!

- **Longer, more complex plots**
- **Popular themes**
- **Lots of characters**
- **A great romance!**

HER SECRET, HIS CHILD

Tara Taylor Quinn

Available May 1999 at your favorite retail outlet.

HARLEQUIN®
Makes any time special ™

Look us up on-line at: http://www.romance.net

HSR4TO6

Which cowboy will become the first daddy in Cactus, Texas?

Cal, Spence, Tuck and Mac have to beware!
Their moms want grandchildren—and these
conniving matchmakers will stop at
nothing to turn their cowboy
sons into family men.

Judy Christenberry's
4 TOTS FOR 4 TEXANS
is another winner!

ONE HOT DADDY-TO-BE?
#773, May 1999

SURPRISE—YOU'RE A DADDY!
#777, June 1999

DADDY UNKNOWN
#781, July 1999

THE LAST STUBBORN COWBOY
#785, August 1999

4 TOTS for 4 TEXANS

Available wherever Harlequin books are sold.

HARLEQUIN®
Makes any time special ™

Look us up on-line at: http://www.romance.net   HAR4TF4T

HARLEQUIN®

AMERICAN ◆ ROMANCE®

Won't you welcome our NEW ARRIVALS

Join us for a nine-month adventure as a soon-to-be mom meets the man of her dreams—and finds a daddy in the bargain—in each book in the New Arrivals promotion.

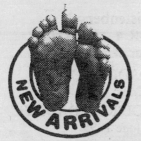

Look for

#784 AND BABIES MAKE TEN
by Lisa Bingham
July 1999

NEW ARRIVALS
We're expecting!

Available wherever Harlequin books are sold.

HARLEQUIN®
Makes any time special™

Look us up on-line at: http://www.romance.net

HARNA2

#777 SURPRISE—YOU'RE A DADDY! by Judy Christenberry
4 Tots for 4 Texans
Spence Hauk never forgot that night when he made love to Melanie Rule.
She was everything he'd wanted, even though she was in love with another
man. But now that Melanie is carrying his child, the rugged cowboy wants
his family—baby *and* wife.

#778 COWBOY IN A TUX by Mary Anne Wilson
Delaney's Grooms
Cowboy J. T. Watson disliked weddings—some years ago he'd been the
groom in one that lasted one night. But this cowboy's on a run of bad
luck when his ex, Candice, ends up his partner at his friend's nuptials...
and he finds a message in his tux that says, "You're still married!"

#779 DIAMOND DADDIES by Linda Cajio
Every man's greatest fortune is his family. Only, twin brothers and
confirmed bachelors Jeff and Julian Diamond don't know it yet. So their
matchmaking grandfather is determined to make sure they have incentive
to marry and give him grandbabies—plus a hefty tax break—by the end
of the year.

#780 STUD FOR HIRE? by Debbi Rawlins
When a stranger tried to hire Adam Knight to romance her "poor,
heartbroken" friend, Adam said "No way!" But the next thing he knew,
"poor" Gracie Allen had stolen his heart. Would she ever believe it when
she learned his secret?

Look us up on-line at: http://www.romance.net

HARLEQUIN · CELEBRATES

In June 1999 Harlequin Presents® gives you
Wedded Bliss—a great new 2-in-1 book
from popular authors
Penny Jordan & Carole Mortimer
2 stories for the price of 1!
Join us as we celebrate Harlequin's 50th anniversary!

Look for these other
Harlequin Presents® titles
in June 1999 wherever
books are sold:

HER GUILTY SECRET
(#2032) by Anne Mather

THE PRICE OF A BRIDE
(#2033) by Michelle Reid

ACCIDENTAL BABY
(#2034) by Kim Lawrence

THE GROOM'S REVENGE
(#2035) by Kate Walker

SLEEPING WITH THE
BOSS (#2036) by
Cathy Williams

Look us up on-line at: http://www.romance.net   H50HP/L